DEBUTANTE

MADELINE MOORE

mischief

This novel is entirely a work of fiction.
The names, characters and incidents portrayed in it are
the work of the author's imagination. Any resemblance to
actual persons, living or dead, events or localities is
entirely coincidental.

Mischief
An imprint of HarperCollins*Publishers*
77–85 Fulham Palace Road,
Hammersmith, London W6 8JB

www.mischiefbooks.com

A Paperback Original 2013

First published in Great Britain in ebook format by
HarperCollins*Publishers* 2012

Copyright © Madeline Moore 2013

Madeline Moore asserts the moral right to
be identified as the author of this work

A catalogue record for this book is
available from the British Library

ISBN-13: 9780007553204

Find out more about HarperCollins and the environment at
www.harpercollins.co.uk/green

CONTENTS

Contents

Chapter One

Emily dropped her robe. She willed herself not to blush as Luke, sprawled naked across his bed, stared at her with the same amazed expression of awe that always crossed his face when she disrobed. His pupils dilated until they were black with mere rims of blue.

She blushed. It was ridiculous to try not to – like trying not to hiccup. It couldn't be done. Emily should be pleased he was so enamoured of her body. She *was* pleased. It wasn't like she wished he'd get used to it or that she suspected he only loved her for her looks. She knew better. She'd been with good boys and bad boys but she'd never been with one like Luke.

Like right now. Any other guy would say, 'Come here,' or at least beckon with an index finger or pat the bed. But he didn't. He just smiled, his eyes black and his impressive manhood already half-erect. He waited, as he had in the restaurant where she'd worked when they met. At some point during every shift he'd show up, not saying a word, just drinking his coffee and eating his toast and watching her work with unconcealed, non-predatory pleasure.

She was used to being hit on. This was LA and everyone was a producer or a director or an agent or a wannabe – a liar, or a gonnabe – a film student. He was a film student. Once in a while he'd frame her with his thumbs and index fingers but to his credit he seemed to be trying to do it when she wasn't looking, not waiting to be sure she was.

Anyway she was a film student too, sort of. Secretly. But it was different for Emily because LA was her home-town. It made sense, economically, to go to university in her home state. And, technically at least, she was a business major. It was only by working as a waitress three nights a week that she'd been able to declare a double major, studying film, too, because she wanted to, not because, like so many *artistes* she'd met, because she had to.

She was interested in 'The Business', all right, but it had nothing to do with appearing in front of the camera.

'You oughta be in pictures,' her customers would say, grinning to let her know that they knew it was a cliché.

'Maybe,' she'd reply, topping up their cups of coffee, 'but I ain't gonna be.'

There was something magical about the movies, that was for sure. You couldn't live here and not feel it, breathe it, know it to be true. But Emily would never be 'in' film. Not like they meant, anyway. Simply put, she was too shy.

She could sing, dance and act her little heart out, in the quiet of her own apartment. But put her on a stage and she became a mannequin – the quintessential 'dumb blonde'. It was beyond horrible.

Just thinking about it made her feel queasy. But she wasn't acting, not now. Now she was scurrying to the bed, eager for the encouragement of Luke's arms around her. He didn't just love her for her looks, she *knew* that. But it didn't hurt to be reassured.

Luke pulled a sheet up to cover them both. He pulled her close, so close she could feel his heart beat against her breasts and his long cock hardening against her belly.

'You are so brave,' he murmured.

By now she knew *he* knew how difficult it was for her to stand before him, nude, and allow herself to be adored. Especially here at his house, where there was always someone playing music and someone else watching TV while two or three students passionately argued the merits of Tarantino versus Truffaut or some other pointless comparison. Doors banged. She was never entirely convinced that the 'scarf on the doorknob' (he didn't own a tie and wouldn't buy a lock) was proper protection from intruders. It wasn't easy to ignore the constant noise and stand around naked in a house where a dozen guys and only one girl, a type 'A' film student named Marion who was rarely home, rocked and rolled their way through college life.

Luke always rewarded her with hugs and gentle kisses and he did so now.

'Baby love,' he murmured, kissing her eyelids. 'Beautiful baby.' He kissed her nose, her ears, her neck and finally her mouth. Though her lips parted eagerly his travelled on, licking and kissing her left shoulder, elbow, wrist and each of her fingers.

'You've been baking,' he murmured, 'you taste like honey. Like cinnamon. Where are you hiding your honey and cinnamon cookies?'

Emily laughed. His 'love talk' was silly, the silliest, but somehow he pulled it off.

'I haven't been baking. I don't know how to cook.'

'I think you bake in secret,' he murmured. He switched to her right hand, nibbling her fingers and then mouthing his way up her arm to lick her armpit until she squealed. 'Maybe you made a pudding for me? A creamy, honey-sweet pudding?'

His cock pressed against the length of her thigh. It was a big one: smooth, circumcised, surrounded by a curly black nest of hair, with lovely big balls hanging down. But he'd never hinted that she might be staying with him because of his generous manhood, just as she'd never accused him of loving her for her looks. Their courtship

4

had been slow. Deliberate. They'd known what they were getting into and they had not balked. And now they were there. In love.

'Maybe I'm making a honey pudding right now,' she whispered.

He laughed, low. But he didn't dive for her pussy the way most guys would when issued such a blatant invitation. He kissed her mouth first. He'd kiss her and kiss her until she was almost forced to ask for it. She imagined Luke could make her grovel for sex if he wanted to but he'd never pushed her that far. He likely knew, though she'd never told him, that making her beg would humiliate her past lust and into anger. She'd told him she had a temper but he'd said it was hard to believe. He'd never seen it.

'God.' The words spilled from her mouth as he released it from his. 'Luke ...'

'Mm. More kisses.' He kissed her breasts, back and forth, circling the areola of each before zeroing in on her nipples with the tip of his tongue. As he moved down the bed, the bedclothes moved with him, leaving her exposed. She should pull them up, but that might break the mood, so what the hell, she'd just have to trust the scarf!

She ached. He hadn't touched her pussy but she knew it was soaking wet. It always creamed like crazy when she posed for him, as if it loved what she knew she feared. Or something. Sometimes he spent a long time going down on her but this time, thank God, he didn't.

His lips met hers again. He kissed her as best he could while positioning himself above her. Finally, the tip of his cock slipped inside Emily. She moaned. Her pussy contracted, as if trying to capture what could only be given freely.

'Em ... I love you, Em ...' Luke slid smoothly inside her.

It always surprised her, the way her pussy seemed to widen and lengthen to accept what had, the first time, seemed far too much for her to handle. But she knew, now, that she could take it. In fact, she loved the way he filled her needy little opening and the entire tunnel it led to. She was stuffed with Luke. He knew, now, not to slam into her, because that did hurt. He knew, too, that just because one little hole of hers opened so nicely for him didn't mean another, smaller, tighter one could. Or would.

'Mm. I love you too, I do. I love this, too ...' Emily tried to verbally excite him, though she wasn't talented at dirty talk. He appreciated her efforts though. He appreciated her. She tilted her hips up, using her body to tell him what she couldn't say.

'You're so wet, Em. So wet and hot.' He shifted his weight to his right arm and reached down between them with his left to massage her clit. 'I want to fuck you all day but I want to come so bad.'

His fingers on her clit tilted her immediately over the edge. The rippling spasms that had seemed to grasp at him now clenched his cock like a fist, opening and closing rhythmically. The orgasm shot through her, making her toes point and her hands splay. It seemed to exit through her open mouth in a long, loud shriek.

Luke rode her through most of it before his eyes screwed shut and his mouth dropped open. He trembled all over as he came, thrusting and softening at the same time, moaning her name.

'Jesus Christ.' He collapsed on top of her.

'Oomph.' Emily's mouth, still open, expelled all the air in her lungs as she took his full weight.

'Sorry,' he muttered. He almost rolled to his left, then rolled to his right instead. He slid his right arm under her neck. 'Sometimes I think, you know, that it's gonna kill me.'

Emily laughed. 'Yeah.'

'You too?' He looked surprised.

'Uh-huh. It's so intense.'

'Think it's because we're in love? Or is it chemistry?'

Emily groaned. 'I don't. I don't think. Please.'

'Sorry.' Luke grinned. He kissed her shoulder.

Emily smiled at him. She loved the way he could change from a take-charge man to a delighted boy. After sex, when his blue eyes were particularly bright and his dark hair was mussed all over, falling into his eyes and standing straight up at the back, in a cowlick, he looked more like a farm boy than a –

An electronic beep sounded.

'What's that?' Emily glanced around lazily.

Luke froze.

'Cell phone needs recharging?' Em stretched. She'd like to catch a nap before work but – she looked at her boyfriend. His eyes were as wide as saucers. As wide as they'd been the first time he saw her breasts. 'What?'

'Nothin'. Must be the cell phone. Let's go downstairs and get some food.'

'I'm not going anywhere.'

The beeping continued.

Luke got out of bed. 'Come on.'

'Luke. What's going on?'

'Nothing. I just –'

Emily propped herself up on her elbow.

She saw it. The blinking red light, just inside his slightly open closet. It could really only be one thing. The problem was she couldn't believe it. She kicked off the covers and got out of bed. It was as if she were on a boat, rocking on the open ocean. She almost stumbled as she headed for the closet.

Luke got there first. He slid the door shut. 'It's nothing,' he whispered.

Emily opened the door. It was a camera, broadcast quality. The battery was low. Hence the beep.

Emily's hand flew to her lips. She stared at Luke. For a moment, they were frozen.

Then all hell broke loose.

Her other hand knocked the camera from its tripod.

'Christ, Em! That belongs to the school!' Luke dived into the closet to rescue the camera.

By the time he emerged she was half-dressed.

'I can explain,' he said.

'Save it.' Emily shot her arms through the sleeves of her sweater. Her hands, as they emerged, were balled into fists. She hadn't bothered to put on her bra; she just grabbed it and stuffed it in her knapsack.

'It's only for me.'

'Liar. You and your pals having a circle jerk watching us "make love"? We're ruined, Luke. You ruined us!'

'No! It's just that you work so many nights and I'm so horny for you and I can't watch porn any more, it doesn't mean anything, it doesn't do anything.'

'You said you never watch porn.'

'I don't. I did, long ago, I guess. But –'

Emily held out her hand.

Luke ejected the tape from the camera and placed it in her palm.

Emily swung her knapsack up onto her back. She opened the door to his room but, instead of leaving, she stood for a moment, facing Luke, her legs slightly apart. She forced some of the confusion and hurt and betrayal and heartsickness to abate so that the rolling rage in her belly concentrated into a dense black ball of hate that she could hurl at Luke and when it was ready, she did.

'I never want to see you again. Don't come to my work or I'll call the cops. Don't ever come to my place. Don't come near me, Luke. We're done. You hear me?'

She raised her fist and shook it at him. The look on his face was one of disbelief. And, yes, fear. Emily squinted her grey eyes and sneered, thus, she hoped, contorting her features into those of an ugly crone.

'If you ever come near me again, I'll tear your balls off and stuff them down your throat.'

She slammed the door behind her when she left.

Chapter Two

Electro house music blasted so loud the old hardwood floors shook. One keg was empty and the second well on its way. This was the last bash before the semester ended and finals, be they on paper or disc, loomed large.

Emily.

Luke emptied the big red cup in his hand and burped. He sat hunched in the left corner of the old maroon sofa, once plush velvet but now matted and in places threadbare, that had been pushed against a wall to make room for dancing. He wanted another beer but the distance between him and the keg seemed vast. He tried to crush the cup and when it merely cracked in his hand, threw it on the floor in disgust.

Disgust. One word encapsulated everything: the house he'd lived in for three years, everyone in the house including his roommates, his stupid ideas for stupid, pretentious movies that would move stupid audiences all over the world. Maybe he needed two words. Stupid.

Disgust. He should get the camera and set it up on the scarred wooden coffee table, aim it at himself and press record. 'Self-portrait of a Stupid, Disgusting Moron.'

The camera, property of the University, was upstairs, hidden from stupid drunks who wouldn't recognise a digital HD camcorder if they fell over it, which they easily could, because they were a bunch of stupid drunks. He'd like to be one of them. Not stupid, he was already that. He'd like to be drunk.

Emily.

'Special delivery.' Marion plopped down beside him and offered him one of the two cups she held. She took a swig from the other. 'Beer. Good.'

Luke gulped a couple of mouthfuls, burped, and agreed. 'Beer. Good.'

'C'mon, Skywalker, let's dance.' Marion nudged him shoulder to shoulder.

She looked every inch the red-hot temptress in a shiny party dress with a pleated skirt and spaghetti straps, its pale green nicely complementing her soft green eyes and henna-red hair. One of those straps slipped down her right shoulder, exposing a little more of her ample cleavage.

Stunning. Luke's lizard brain woke up with a start. It'd been asleep for three weeks and almost resented the intrusion. Almost.

Marion kicked up her heels, which were ridiculously high for a kegger in a house with uneven floors.

'Nope.' Luke gulped his beer.

'You keep drinking like that and you know what's going to happen.'

'I'll pass out?'

'You'll have to pee which means you'll actually have to rise up from the sofa and move your legs.'

'True.' Luke leaned over the frayed armrest and slowly poured the rest of his beer on the floor.

'Hey,' protested Marion, 'who do you think is going to clean that up in the morning?'

'I dunno. But it won't be you.' Luke almost laughed. Marion did not do housework.

She shrugged. The second spaghetti strap slipped down her left shoulder. More cleavage. Lots of cleavage.

Lizard likes cleavage.

Marion drew her knees up and rested them across his thighs. She leaned in close, her thick red hair caressing his cheek, her breasts soft and sexy against his shoulder, her cherry-red lips just touching his ear, 'C'mon, Longfellow, let's go upstairs.'

Luke sighed. Otherwise he didn't move a muscle. Only the slight thickening of his cock down the right side of his jeans let on that Marion was having an effect on him.

'Mmm. We used to be so good together, remember? You with your big fat cock and me a size queen with my big mouth just made to suck?' She rimmed his ear with her tongue. 'We were the perfect friends with benefits.

13

Don't you agree?'

He nodded. There was no point trying to deny it. They'd been a good fit, sexually.

She wriggled onto his lap. Her pleated skirt covered both his legs but she was only interested in the right one, the one with his long cock rising to life against it. Marion split her knees so that they hugged each side of his leg. She rocked, ever so slightly, just enough to caress his denim-covered dick with her naked pussy and press her hard little nipples against his chest.

'Remember when you'd fuck me up the ass? That was my favourite. You liked it, too, didn't you? Man, it wasn't easy getting that mega-cock of yours all the way up my little pink hole but we did it, didn't we?'

'*Assssssssssss*,' hissed the lizard, fully awake now.

Luke was mesmerised. Before Em he'd either had sex or masturbated every single day. Otherwise he couldn't concentrate. Sometimes it was fun and sometimes it was spectacular and sometimes it was as mundane as brushing his teeth. When Marion had moved into the house, in his second year, it'd been like a gift from the gods. A free-spirited, horny little bitch who had a thing for big cocks. They *had* been a good fit. She took the pill but he'd always worn a condom and she'd never complained. Not even when he split her ass cheeks and targeted her puckered hole with his hard-as-a-helmet dick-head.

'Good time ...' she whispered. She licked and kissed

his ear, then started her way down the side of his face to his neck.

He shuddered. He always shuddered when a girl kissed his neck. His cock strained against the fabric of his jeans. Damn. Her hot cunt felt great. She was already so wet he could feel it dampening his jeans and his hard-on beneath them. He needed it so bad. Maybe it was time to face facts. Emily was gone. Gone for good.

'Yesssssssssss,' hissed the lizard.

'No,' said Luke.

'Please, baby, I'm close. Please ...' Marion arched her back, exposing her nipples, bearing down on his leg and the erection trapped against it, tipping up her ass.

'Anal slut.' Luke slipped his hands under her skirt and parted her ass cheeks. 'Beg some more.'

'Please, Luke, please, please.'

He pushed his left index finger into her asshole, ignoring the resistance. 'More. I'm an anal slut and I want more.'

'"I'm an anal slut and I want more ..."' Marion's words slurred together. She pressed her pussy down, jiggling just enough to rub her clit against his cock. 'More you fucking ... fucking ... fuck ...'

Luke bounced his leg and she rose a little. His hands still held her ass cheeks apart but as she bore down on his cock again his second index finger joined the first.

Marion fell forwards, her breasts bracketing his face.

'Uhhhhhhh ...'

'Quiet,' Luke said.

He bounced her again, jamming both fingers as far up inside her as he could. One more little bounce and she'd probably ...

He felt the clenching contractions of her empty pussy through the veil of skin that separated it from her ass and his punishing index fingers. He kept up the rhythm of his fingers but let her grind her cunt against his cock until the spasms slowed and stopped.

'Fuck,' she moaned in his ear.

He tumbled her sideways off his lap.

'Pleazzzzzzzzzzzzzze ...' moaned the lizard.

'Shut up,' said Luke.

He made his way through the crowd and up the stairs.

Two minutes in the bathroom and three weeks of pent-up need spilled into the bowl. He flushed it, washed his hands and lay down on his bed.

Disgust. Stupid. Shut up, Luke.

He buried his face in his pillow and pulled another one over his head to muffle the hateful sound of drunken revelry.

Emily.

Chapter Three

It was a quiet night at Bailey's, the fine dining restaurant where Emily worked, so she spotted Marion as soon as the hostess seated her. Emily had made sure to tell every hostess she worked with to seat a single girl with hair the colour of red velvet in her section, if and when such a person showed up.

Now that Marion was here, Emily was terrified to talk to her. The last time it'd been easy, she'd just sat and shook her head while Marion tried to make various points in Luke's favour.

'Guys his age are always horny. They wake up that way and they go to bed that way. They can't help it,' Marion had said.

'I don't care. He had no right shooting me without my consent.'

'True. But he's sorry. He's a mess, Emily. A total disaster. I think he might not even get his projects finished in time to pass the semester.' (This part was not true; all

Luke did was work on the short movie due by mid-April. But Marion had never had any trouble making up stories and the lie was for a good cause.)

'What about me? I'm doing a double major and I can't concentrate. All I can think of is Luke and his friends watching us fuck.'

Marion had set four more discs on the table. 'He wouldn't do that. Here are the rest of the movies he made of you two. He wants you to have them all. He says he can't stand having them around.'

'He probably already has someone new and he just doesn't want –'

'Nobody new.'

'Because he hasn't had the opportunity.'

'Oh come on. The poor guy's in love with you. I bet he wouldn't have sex with a girl if she threw herself into his lap.'

Which was when they'd made their agreement. Marion was to do her best to try to seduce Luke and report the result back to Emily.

It'd been a tough ten days but now she was here.

Emily delivered the entrées she carried on her tray and gave Rhonda a nod. She hadn't taken many breaks on her last few shifts, with the understanding that when the redhead showed up, she'd take a break immediately.

Rhonda nodded back. Emily slid into the chair opposite Marion.

'Well?'

'What, no how-do-you-do?' Marion grinned.

'Sorry. How are you?' Emily picked up the linen napkin on the table and started absently-mindedly twisting it.

'Fine, thank you. But I can't say the same for your poor old ex. I think all the sperm he's not expelling might be slowly poisoning him. Hey –' she tilted her head sideways, as she always did when she had an idea '– that's not a bad idea for a short.'

'It's dumb.' Emily looked down at the tortured napkin in her hands. When she looked back up, her eyes brimmed with tears.

'C'mon, kiddo,' Marion whispered, 'stop your suffering. And Luke's. Just watching it is painful. Listen, I threw myself at him at that kegger we had. Seriously. I offered him anal –'

'Sssh.' Emily looked around but no one seemed to have heard. 'Really?'

'I gave it everything I've got. No kidding.'

'And?'

'He was nice about it, you know. A real gentleman. I kissed his neck, you know? I even climbed into his lap.'

Emily's eyes narrowed. The visual was not appealing. 'Was he drunk?'

'He'd had a few. Any other guy would've been begging for it. But in this case it was me doing the begging. I had him cornered, on that funky couch we have, and I was

19

all over him. I was like, "Please, Luke, I'm desperate, I need that big cock of yours so bad, baby, I'll do anything you want" and –'

'Get to the fucking point already.'

'He turfed me off his lap and said, "Shut up." Then he went upstairs and never came back.' Marion held out her hands, palms up. 'The dude's in love with you, Emily.'

Hope bloomed like a rose in Emily's heart. She felt the heat of happiness rise from her chest until her cheeks flushed with it and it her eyes overflowed with it and she wept into her shredded napkin.

'So can he come see you?'

Emily nodded. 'Tomorrow. My place. Eight p.m.'

'Good girl.' Marion slid from her chair. She patted Emily awkwardly on the shoulder.

Emily looked up at her. 'Thanks, Marion.' She wiped her cheeks.

'Aw,' muttered Marion, seemingly embarrassed by her good deed. 'It was nothing.'

'I owe you one,' said Emily. But before she could stand up and give Marion a hug, the other girl was gone.

Some people were funny that way; couldn't handle gratitude. But she wouldn't forget. She owed Marion and someday, somehow, she'd pay her back.

Chapter Four

Luke stuck his key into Emily's lock. He tentatively tried the door and, when it opened, heaved a sigh of relief so complete it caused a full-body shudder. He'd hardly dared hope Marion was telling the truth when she'd said Emily wanted to see him. But she hadn't locked the dead bolt to keep him out.

Dead Bolt. Not a bad name for a short. He gave his head a shake. He didn't need to think about film any more. He was finished, as far as third year was concerned. But, more importantly, he wasn't all that interested in the subject. For the first time in his life, something mattered more than making movies. Right here. Right now. This was the most important moment of his life.

'Emily?'

No answer. He checked his cell phone. Eight p.m. on the nose. He'd followed Marion's instructions to the letter. He was about to call out again when he heard a soft moan coming from Emily's bedroom.

The door was ajar. He pushed it open. The sight that met his eyes was astonishing.

Em was lying in bed, naked and uncovered. The movie, their movie, the one that had caused all the fuss, was playing on her TV. The sound was turned down low but he could hear their voices, thick with lust. He could see the purity of their love in the way they looked at each other, in their kisses and caresses. It was a heady combination.

'Em?' He stood in the doorway, unsure of his next move.

She looked over her shoulder. Her face was flushed and her grey eyes were as misty as a seaside morning. Damp blonde curls framed her face.

Her beauty left him speechless. He ventured into the room. Now he could see that she was toying with her nipples while her right hand stroked her pussy.

'Help me?' Emily's voice was so sweet he could almost taste it. She turned her attention back to the TV.

Luke stripped. He crawled onto the bed until he was pressed up against her back. He reached around her hip to place his right hand over hers.

In unison their two hands teased and pleased her sopping wet pussy. At his touch, she'd begun to shudder. It wasn't going to take long.

Luke gently tucked the damp curls on her cheek behind her ear. He licked the sweat from her face and neck.

When he spoke on the screen, he whispered the same words in her ear. 'Em … I love you, Em …'

Emily trembled from head to toe. She joined him in repeating the words she said on tape. 'Mm. I love you too, I do. I love this, too.'

His hard-on rubbed her spine. He slid lower to take her from behind. '… so wet, Em. So wet and hot …'

Luke slid smoothly inside her warm, welcoming pussy, the sheath to a sword that was back from away. He fucked her in long, slow strokes while covering her hand with his, applying extra pressure to her fingers on her clit.

She moaned, still shaking from head to toe.

He licked her cheek. Tears mingled with sweat. His eyes blurred with tears, too. '… come so bad …'

For a moment Emily seemed to freeze. The trembling ceased as she stilled, a warm ivory statue wet with rain.

'Go for it,' whispered Luke. 'It's yours, baby. Take it.'

She let out a strangled shriek and then another, not so strangled.

Luke pressed his palm against hers, mashing her clit as he fucked her through the grasping spasms of her orgasm and on into the grand release of his.

The short film was over. But Luke was still shuddering, spurting weakly inside her, when she groped for the remote and powered off the TV.

Finally, both were still.

He slipped free of her.

'I watched them all,' she said. 'They're love tapes.'

'Yeah!' A part of him swelled with pride. She'd finally seen what he'd been sure he'd captured. 'But we can get rid of them. I can –'

'No. I … I like them. I want to make more.'

She rolled over, wrapped her arms around him and burst into tears. 'Never leave me again,' she said. A small, balled fist whacked his shoulder for emphasis.

'I won't,' he said. Tears slid down his face and he made no attempt to hide them. Nor did he choose to remind her who had left who. It didn't matter.

Nothing mattered. Emily was his again.

Not only that, but she wanted to make more tapes. His cock twitched at the thought. Add to that the fact that he'd finished his third year of film school and his world was complete.

What could possibly go wrong?

Chapter Five

The Film Department was in a frenzy. Students wandered the halls as if lost and one girl had thrown up her hands in dismay before bursting into tears. She stood, sobbing, among scattered papers, text books and discs.

Emily stood at the front entrance to the building, panting. She'd just run from Business, almost across the entire campus, with her knapsack bouncing on her back. The halls should be close to empty, but it looked like practically no one had gone to class. She spotted Marion, her face white beneath her unruly mop of crimson hair.

'What?' said Emily.

'They just informed us that tuition is going up forty per cent.'

Emily's shoulders slumped. Her knapsack thumped on the floor.

'You've got to be –' She'd been about to say 'kidding' but it was obvious from the scene before her eyes that this was no joke. 'The whole University?'

'Nope. Just Film. How do you like that?'

'Can they do that? Is it even legal?'

'The University's been threatening it for years. You know that. Cost of this, cost of that … and now it's done. Starts in September. I'm screwed. We're all screwed. Except for you, I guess.'

'What makes you say that?'

'Don't you have some fat trust fund you can dip into any time you like?'

'Yeah, I only schlep plates three nights a week for the fun of it. I'm studying for a part because when I graduate I really want to play a waitress.'

Marion shrugged.

Emily spotted Luke and dragged her knapsack across the floor until she reached him. Like the others, he was stuck in freeze frame.

She gave his arm a shake. 'Snap out of it, Luke. C'mon.'

Luke followed her like a robot, down the hall and out of the building. She stopped at the bus stop.

'Do you have any money?' she asked.

'Some. Where are we going?'

'To see my stepmom,' Emily said.

'What for?'

'To try to talk her into letting me have access to my "fat trust fund",' she replied grimly.

It was a short bus ride to Beverly Hills. Emily peppered Luke with instructions but she could tell most of it wasn't getting through to him. It was her own fault. She'd chosen to keep her life story to herself, easily deflecting his questions by asking her own questions about him. As a result, she knew plenty about his childhood in Brentwood, Vermont: mom, dad, two older sisters and a little brother, happy, middle class, everyone loved going to the movies on a Saturday night. All Luke knew about her was that she came from money, didn't remember her long-dead mother, did remember her much-loved late father and barely saw her stepmother.

Emily stopped talking. Luke stared forlornly out the window, as if seeing LA for the last time. It had been a mistake to bring him along, she saw that now. But it was too late.

She tugged at his arm. 'Luke. Listen to me.'

'That was fun last night, huh?' He gave her a wan smile.

Emily nodded. Ever since their magical make-up sex they'd experimented with shooting their lovemaking sessions. With a few mirrors, decent lighting and proper sound equipment, they'd made some seriously steamy little movies. It had taken surprisingly little time for her to get used to the idea that her naked body and Luke's, engaged in the most intimate acts possible between two people, with all the accompanying sucks and licks and moans and orgasmic howls, was being recorded.

'You're a good film-maker, Luke,' she said.

'Nah. It's you, Em. You're as pretty as a porn star.'

Emily blushed, oddly pleased by a comment that would've made her mad as hell a month ago. She jumped up. 'Come on. This is our stop.'

It was a long walk from the stop to her house. She tried, again, to get a couple of facts hammered into his head, but he'd gone from glum to dazed.

'Bobby mustn't know about the film-making course, Luke. Got that?'

'Fuck me. Look at that place. It's a palace!'

'Luke!'

'Right. Bobby mustn't know – hey, why do you call her Bobby, anyway?'

'I had a deviated septum when I was little. I couldn't say "Mommy", I said "Bobby". The nickname stuck even after I had surgery when I was twelve.'

'So that's why you have a perfect schnoz.' Luke ran his finger down her admittedly perfect nose.

'Yeah but it wasn't, like, a nose job, I mean it wasn't cosmetic, it was – look, it's not important, Luke. What's important is that you remember not to let on that I'm studying Film as well as Business. OK?'

He shrugged. 'Sure.' He gazed around. 'Jeez, can you imagine shooting in this place? Look at the ultra-cool shadows those palm trees cast on that stone path – what kind of stone sparkles like that? So where's home sweet home?'

Inwardly, Emily groaned. 'This is it,' she said.

28

'Holy shit.'

'Oh and try not to swear. Please, Lukey? Please.'

'Holy cow.'

It was an impressive house on a block of impressive houses. An unexpected surge of pride made Emily straighten her back and raise her chin. This was where she'd grown up.

The sloping roof of the bungalow was red; her dad had been one of the very first residents to install solar panels. It was a bit of a climb up the stone walkway and each level offered bright bursts of colourful flowers among overgrown shiny green bushes. The double doors were flanked by huge bay windows. Above the doors, a smaller lead glass window completed the voluptuous, yet cosy, façade of the manse.

Emily pointed to the little window. 'My room.'

'Fuuuuck,' whispered Luke.

Her heart sank.

They hadn't taken three steps into the foyer before a slender, tanned woman in figure-hugging Capris and a peasant blouse emerged from the kitchen.

'Who's there?'

Emily dropped her knapsack and opened her arms. 'Bobby!'

'My God, girl, you gave me a scare.' Even after over a decade in the States, her voice was still flavoured by a delicious hint of her original Brazilian accent.

Bobby enveloped Emily in a long, hard hug.

'Mm. You smell good,' said Emily. 'I miss you.' She loved the feel of Bobby's skinny arms around her but at the same time, being breast to breast, her stepmom braless as always, felt a bit awkward. That, in turn, made her feel guilty. Moms are supposed to be sexless in their children's eyes. Shouldn't it be the same for stepmoms? Somehow, for Emily, with Bobby, it wasn't, but then Bobby hadn't come along until Emily was ten. Did that make a difference? It didn't help that Bobby was all touchy-feely; if you were within reach, she had a hand on you. The house boasted a state-of-the-art sauna, but Emily had never used it, just in case Bobby decided to join her. She wriggled free of her stepmother's arms.

'You didn't tell me you were coming,' Bobby accused. 'I would have ordered some food. Students are always hungry, yes?' She squinted her warm caramel eyes at Luke.

He nodded helplessly.

'Sorry. It was kind of an impulse thing,' said Emily.

'Good impulse. Have it more often, please.' She turned her full attention to Luke, crossing her arms under her voluptuous breasts. 'And who's the handsome boy?'

'A friend. You always say you want to meet my friends.'

Bobby lifted a thin eyebrow. 'Friend or *friend*?'

'Don't embarrass him,' Emily scolded.

'Don't worry. I'm no prude. I know how it is these days with college kids. Friends with benefits, huh?'

'Real life isn't like TV,' Emily defended. 'We're much more than friends.'

'But you are not engaged?' She grabbed Emily's left hand and, seeing no ring, let it go. 'Never mind. Your father and I, we were not engaged.' She focused on Luke again. 'For us it was love at first sight. He was in my country, looking for tin. You know – minering.'

'Mining,' corrected Emily.

'And me – I was young. I was looking only for fun. But we met and – poof! A month later we were married.' She touched her fingertips to the inside rims of her eyes. Her left ring finger sported a brilliant diamond set in yellow gold. 'Daniel gave me this,' she said, flashing her ring at Luke.

'Awesome,' he managed to squeak.

Emily tried not to cringe. She refused to be embarrassed by the man she loved.

'He say if I come to America we can live anywhere I want. "Oh I want to live in Hollywood," I say. It is the only place I know about, in America. From the movies. Can you imagine?'

Luke nodded. 'I love LA,' he said.

Emily interrupted. 'Bobby –' she began.

'I know, we must not dwell.' She blinked rapidly, her lashes, thick and long as little brushes, drying her eyes. 'We were very happy family, no?'

'Yes,' said Emily. 'We … we still are.'

Bobby flashed a brilliant grin. 'True. Now, your young man will please remove his rucksack and I will tell him, "My name is not really Bobby but you may call me Bobby anyway," and I will call you –?'

'Luke.' He dumped his knapsack and extended his hand.

Bobby took it and pulled him into an embrace. 'Luke! I like this name. May the farce be with you, no?'

'I guess …' He nodded against her neck, his furiously blushing face mostly hidden by her thick black curtain of hair. He shot Emily a helpless glance.

Emily had to laugh. 'Come on, let's go sit by the pool,' she said, tugging Luke free.

Bobby dismissed the idea with a wave of her hand. 'I have closed the pool. If I go out for a dip or a little topless tanning the neighbours flee into their houses. Americans – so *up*tight. We go sit in the kitchen, OK?' She turned and walked away, hips swinging. 'You want coffee, you have to make it. I don't know how to drive the machine.'

'Mary's day off?' Emily asked.

'Mary? She's not with me any more. I manage for myself, for now.'

'What happened to your little job at the spa?' asked Emily. Mary had been a fixture in the house since before she could remember. The only reason Bobby would possibly have let her go would be lack of money. 'Are we OK?'

'So many questions.' Bobby frowned. 'I admit it will be good when you finish business school so you can help me understand what is what is what with these mining stocks and companies and corporations and etcetera.'

'Really? Because I was thinking I could help you now if –'

'Shush. You are a student now. We wait. But that spa! Oh my God! I am making mani/pedis and seaweed wrap and hot stone massage but no, now the ladies want to have the –' she lowered her voice as if this would prevent Luke from hearing '– the back entrance bleached! This is disgusting, no? And they want ... how is it said ... bejewelled vaginas. Phooey! I have to do this or I have to go so –' she shrugged '– I go. Make frothy coffee, please.'

Emily was no *barista* but she could work an espresso machine. Luke didn't embarrass her by asking for milk, thank goodness. He really wasn't so gauche. It was just Emily being ashamed of her privileged background. Reverse snobbery was an insidious thing.

They sat around the island counter and sipped, nibbling the slightly stale cookies that Bobby served from a tin.

'So,' Bobby asked, 'what have you come to tell me, Emily? This boy get you pregnant?'

'No!' Emily blurted a fraction faster than Luke.

'Good. So we got that out of the way. What's next?'

She counted on a finger. 'You gay and coming out to me?' After a pause, she looked at Luke and said, 'I don't think so. Not with a friend like this one. What next? Or maybe you just tell me and don't make me keep guessing? How would that be for an idea, huh?'

'It's money,' Emily confessed. 'I need more.'

'Hmm. I must try to live on the monies from your daddy and you must do the same. Life is so expensive now! But you got everything paid for, out of your trust, and you got pocket money. You've always been good with money, so, how come you need more? Want me to start guessing again?'

'No, no, that won't be necessary,' Emily interrupted. 'I just – I'm twenty-one and I think it's time for you to give me my trust fund. I can help you with the companies, Bobby. And I want to manage my own life.'

'But that is not what your father stop– step– *stipu*-lates in his will. I know you know what he wants. After you graduate from any programme *but* movie programme, *then* you will get your money.' Bobby squinted over her coffee cup. 'If you need more money you can work, no?'

'She works three nights a week already,' said Luke. 'With her course load –'

Emily shot him a look so hard he recoiled as if she'd slapped his face.

'Sorry,' he said. 'Fuck.' He grimaced. 'Sorry.'

'Oh, this word I hear everywhere all the time! Not in my house, do you hear me?'

Luke nodded. He hunched over his coffee cup.

Bobby turned eyes that were suddenly icy on her step-daughter. 'Why you are working? Why do you want your money now?'

'Tuition is going up, way up,' said Emily.

'No it isn't. I got the statement last week. You're paid up for next year already. Now, tell me the truth, and don't break my heart with lies.'

Bobby had always had the knack of punishing Emily with guilt. Emily had never been grounded or had her allowance cut off, growing up. She'd just had to live with breaking her stepmother's heart on a fairly regular basis.

And this time she was really guilty! What could she do except …

Emily burst into gut-wrenching sobs.

Luke grabbed her hand and squeezed it but kept his mouth closed. Bobby waited. That wasn't what she was supposed to do. She was supposed to embrace Emily and forgive her for everything, even if she didn't know what 'everything' was.

Eventually, Emily gulped the last of her sobs back and straightened her back.

'Now tell me,' Bobby ordered.

'I've been bad,' Emily said.

'How bad?'

'I've lied to you.'

'That much I know already. Now the truth, if you remember what that is.'

'I'm doing a double major. You get the statement for one and I get the statement for the other. I pay for it myself. It's another business course.'

'Which you need to keep a secret from me, why?'

Emily mumbled, 'The business of film.'

'I can't hear you.'

'The business of film.'

'Meaning what?'

'How to be a movie producer.'

'Cool,' said Luke. 'I thought you wanted to write.'

'And executive produce, Luke.'

'Hey, we could really –'

Bobby picked up her coffee cup, inspected it carefully, and hurled it across the room where it smashed into the sink. '*That* is what you've done to my heart. You know how your poor father felt about that Hollywood nonsense!' She looked at the ceiling, fist raised, clenched and shaking, 'You hear your daughter, Daniel? Forgive her, if you can. Blame me. I should have made you move us away from this goddam town. Turn your hate on me, my beloved, just so that you forgive your only daughter, no matter what she has become.'

She turned to Emily. 'Your tuition is paid. Your allowance is fixed. Not another penny, though, not until you come into your trust. When you have graduated. From your business course.' She grabbed Luke's arm and gave it a shake. 'I suppose you are going to be our new Johnny Depp, hm? Or Brad Pitt, maybe?'

'No. I plan to direct,' said Luke.

'Let go of him,' said Emily.

Bobby released Luke's arm and focused on her step-daughter once more. 'Not a dropped crumb from under my table. Not a drop of water from my well.'

'Your well, from *my* father. Maybe it's run dry, Bobby? No Mary? Garden overgrown? No pool man? I've never known you not to have a pool man. Tell me the truth. Are you cashing in my companies and spending my money?'

'How dare you!' Bobby grasped the gauzy fabric of her peasant blouse, either feigning a heart attack or about to rend her clothing in despair, Emily wasn't sure. Nor did she care.

'Let's get out of here, Luke.'

Bobby shrieked at them from the kitchen as they hoisted their knapsacks on. '*Nothing* from me, no, not even my love, until you come to your senses and crawl back to me, begging forgiveness. Then, we shall see. Now go!'

They trudged to the bus stop in silence. Emily would've cried had she not already burst into tears a scant half-hour earlier.

It wasn't until they were on the bus back to campus that Luke spoke up. 'What's the big deal, Emily? What did your dad have against the movie business?'

Emily sighed. 'I never knew. At a guess, I'd say he lost money investing in a movie sometime, but that doesn't seem enough to make him so prejudiced. He wasn't a fanatic. We went to the movies and watched movies, but we never *talked* about them or the making of them. As far as he was concerned, everyone in the business side of film was really, really evil. If he'd known I wanted to become a producer someday, it'd be like I was embracing the devil – or worse.'

Luke hugged her. 'Well, we've all got our quirks.'

'This one,' Emily said, 'might cost me my family or my career, or both.'

Chapter Six

Emily stood in the doorway of The Muggery, waiting for her eyes to adjust to the dim interior of the huge bar. She and Luke had had great times in the Film students' favourite drinking establishment. Now it looked like the good times were over, forever. Luke and the others were at the back. She could see them glumly slurping from their mugs. The plan was to 'brainstorm' a solution to their financial woes. In Emily's opinion, that was just talk. In the real world, dreams weren't enough. Her own last hope had been that she'd be allowed to transfer the payment of her Business course to her Movie one. Sure she could. All she needed was her trustee's signature. Fat chance!

The Movie Mob occupied the bar's back room, by leave of a proprietor who fancied himself as a future producer. He always had funds 'almost secured' but they never arrived. Every Film student who met him got excited about Eric's promises of employment, 'once things gelled', at first. Eventually reality sank in. Eric was a wannabe who never would be, but he meant well. Best of all, if you went along with his dreams, you got to run a tab and yesterday's stale pretzels were free.

The jugs of lager on the big back room table were all half empty. A dozen young faces lifted to greet Emily expectantly. She shrugged and shook her head.

Luke said, 'Fuck!'

Emily slumped into a chair.

As if on the other end of a seesaw, Marion jumped up. It was amazing how resilient that girl was. Someday, Emily was sure, Marion would amount to something. She was too fizzy to keep bottled up.

Short skirt swinging, long legs flashing, Marion stepped from her chair onto the table. That got everyone's, particularly the boys', attention.

'Are we defeated?' Marion wanted to know.

Someone at the back grunted, 'Yes,' but Marion ignored him.

'We've got a roomful of talent here,' she went on. 'All we need is some money.'

That brought another groan from the back.

'Shut up!' Marion ordered. 'You want to enjoy the leg show?' She pulled her hem higher up one thigh. 'Then you've gotta show some enthusiasm, OK?'

'We're all enthused about your legs, Marion,' Luke assured her.

Emily poked his ribs with her elbow but only in fun. She had no problem with his admiring other women, from a distance. Not even this one.

Marion gave Luke a warm smile. 'OK, we don't have much cash, but we must have assets of some sort, no? I suggest that we pool everything we've got.'

'All for one and one for all,' Jillian contributed. Diminutive and curvaceous, the bouncy brunette always played cheerleader to Marion. Emily suspected there was a little girl-crush going on there. It fascinated her.

'Exactly,' Marion said. 'And united we stand, and so on. So, who's for pooling our resources?'

One by one, hands rose, except for Guy's. They all knew that he was on the point of failing his course, so that was understandable. He crept from the room, followed by good wishes.

Marion slipped the silver bracelet she always wore off her wrist and held it high. 'I pledge this genuine Navajo bracelet to the Gods of Film. Help us in our hour of need!'

With that, she returned to her seat, leaving the bracelet in the middle of the table.

Jillian took out a pad and pen.

Emily watched as Jillian carefully printed: *One Navajo bracelet*. She knew the bracelet would not make as much as a dint in the cost of the tuition hike for a dozen students. However, Marion's dramatic presentation had raised everyone's spirits and that certainly counted for something.

Marion announced, 'I've got almost a thousand bucks in my savings. I'll pledge that, too.' She was cheered and her pledge neatly noted by Jillian. 'Who's next?'

By the time they were done there was a pitiful pile of valuables on the table and a pledge of almost two thousand dollars. Jillian reported that among them, so far, they could cover the increase in one student's tuition, with enough left over for a hamburger with fries.

Faces fell. A couple got up and headed for the door.

Marion said, 'Wait a minute! That's just our material assets. We have more.'

Someone asked, 'Like what?'

Marion looked at Emily. 'OK to tell them?' she asked.

'Tell them what?'

'About your very valuable assets, that cost you nothing and are renewable.'

It took Emily a few moments to work out what Marion was referring to. 'Do you mean –?'

'Exactly.'

Emily looked at Luke, who was red in the face but nodded. 'Go ahead,' she told Marion.

'OK, everyone. Just for their own amusement, Emily and Luke have been making private movies. Very private, if you know what I mean.'

All faces turned to Emily and Luke.

'If we knew where to sell that sort of thing, I bet they'd fetch a fortune.' She looked at Emily. 'Not yours, of course. I'm talking about new, specially shot, movies.'

'Thank you for that,' Emily said.

'We have Luke to direct,' Marion said. 'Emily could produce. I'll write.'

'I hope to do some of the writing as well,' said Em, swiftly taking control of the situation back from Marion. 'But mainly, I'll be executive producer. Anyone got a problem with that?'

No one did.

Pointing to the students in turn, she said, 'Lighting. Sound. Camera. You two big guys, grips? Everything else, we can double up on, except … talent!' She looked around the room. The men she'd appointed as grips raised their hands.

'Good. Are you equipped for the job? Well equipped?'

One dropped his. The other, bald-headed, well over six feet tall, dark-skinned with chiselled features, looked like he wanted to say something. He seemed vaguely familiar.

Emily raised a brow at him. 'What?'

'Just in case, I'm training as a camera operator.' His voice was deep and resonant, enough to vibrate Emily's spine.

'That makes you our second camera, then,' she said, 'if we ever get the chance to use two. You don't mind being a grip?'

'No problem. I'm behind you one hundred per cent, Emily. I'll help out any way I can, even in front of the camera.'

'Thanks …?'

'Paul. I live with Luke and Marion and Richard and Tony and Jimmy and –'

Emily bit her lip. 'Sorry, Paul. I won't forget your name again.'

Paul shook his head in mock despair. 'I'm the only black dude in the house, Emily.'

'Excuse me for being colour blind,' Emily retorted. She flashed him her best apologetic grin.

Everyone, including Paul, cracked up.

Emily pressed on. 'Talking about performing, I hope everyone took advantage of that free fancy STI test the school offered last month?'

Most heads nodded.

Gary said, 'Kara and I are monogamous. We didn't do it.'

'Luke and I are monogamous, too, but we thought it was a good idea. If you can still get it for free, do, OK? Otherwise we'll pay for it. That goes for everyone. Not that I'm expecting to shoot an orgy anytime soon. I propose that the actors on camera are already couples in real life – or triples, or, for those who are willing, at least good friends. Still, I think the tests are a good idea.'

Heads nodded.

'I'll fuck pretty much whoever,' said Marion, 'if you think I qualify in the looks department.'

Emily recalled Luke's compliment from the other day. 'You're as pretty as any porn star, Marion.'

Jillian piped up. 'What about me?'

'You too,' Emily assured her. 'Am I right, guys?'

The men assented with gusto.

'Then I'm in,' Jillian announced. She shrugged. 'I just want to act.'

'Thanks, Jillian. Who else? Couples, want to talk it over between yourselves and make joint decisions?'

Kara, exotic and raven-haired, said, 'Gary and me are in, provided it doesn't get too kinky.'

'There's no such thing as "too kinky" by me,' Jillian said, surprising Em.

'So where do we start, Emily?' Marion asked.

Right. *Christ!* As E.P., everything fell on her. Failure or success, it was on her shoulders. She'd be making all the major decisions, every one of them vital.

'We'll need a company registered, to make us legit. I'll look into buying a shell.'

Blaine piped up. 'My dad'll give me one.'

'Great,' said Emily. 'We need it now.'

The rest of the group looked puzzled.

'Don't worry about this business stuff,' Emily said. She nodded to Jillian. 'Write it down.'

Emily's mind was whirring like the blades of a

helicopter. She'd been planning to start a film company as soon as she graduated. So why not start right now? OK, maybe producing porn hadn't been the plan but these days it was crucial to be flexible. This thing could actually work!

'Equipment is major, which means we have to have one of us enrolled in a summer course, on the technical side of things. Luke, you've been pretty inventive in spiriting equipment in and out of the department. We'll get you signed up for a course.'

Luke nodded.

'I can help in that department,' said Patricia. 'Professor Simmons and I ...'

'I knew it! All those freakin' top marks for that hand-held camera work of yours. I thought I was gonna have a seizure if I had to watch any more of it,' Marion said.

Patricia shrugged. 'He likes that documentary-style shit. And me.'

'It can work. Look at *Blair Witch Project*,' said Luke.

'*District 9*,' piped up Gary.

'Tarantino says –' began Richard.

'THANK YOU, Patricia,' shouted Emily. Sometimes, she wondered if ADD was a requirement for the film programme.

'Don't forget post-production, Em,' said Luke.

'Right. Editor?'

Richard, one of Luke's roommates, held up his hand.

'Sound editor.' Emily pointed at Marion. 'I guess that'll have to include music and special effects. OK?'

'Great. I have my own recording gear but we'll need to use the Film Department's editing equipment if we want a polished product.'

Richard nodded his agreement.

'As long as Luke's taking a course we should be OK. After that ...' Emily glanced pointedly at Patricia.

'I have a key,' she said. 'Maybe I'll forget to return it after the semester ends.'

'Thank you again, Patricia. Please, people, listen up. We've got a month before the end of the semester,' she continued. 'We can start as soon as we have scripts – and I mean real scripts. That's what's going to make our stuff stand out from the crap on the internet.'

'Stories,' said Marion.

'Yeah, but not just stories. Love stories,' said Em.

The group erupted in a cacophony of discussion. Emily waited them out.

'I'm no actress,' she began, 'but the stuff Luke and I have made is – and I really mean this, as a person who has trained for three years to spot the gem in the rubble – it's powerful. Because we're in love.' She paused to take a sip of her beer. Everyone waited in silence. Good. She took the time to gather her energy, her intention and her intellect. She felt the moment when the alchemy of the combined elements began to flow from her gut upwards, outwards, infusing her entire body with confidence, and she began.

'We start with offering three choices. "Couples in Love" is the first. It'll be easy to write and my apartment is already set up for it. We could have the series in the can before the end of semester.'

From the corner of her eye, she saw Luke watching her intently. The unabashed pride on his face made her ego swell. Good. She needed the ego of Lex Luthor to pull this thing off.

She continued, 'The second line would be "Love on the Run", the idea being that even chance encounters can be meaningful. A one-night stand doesn't have to be cheap. Know what I mean?'

A few people nodded, Marion among them. Em knew Luke could squeeze the performance out of his actors, if they were willing to give it a shot. So to speak.

'By then, we should be generating income. Then we hit them with "Share and Share Alike". For those actors who are willing, of course.'

She focused on Marion. 'Those scripts will be particularly delicate to write because I still want them to emphasise love. We've all heard of threesomes, right? Who's heard of polyamory?'

Most of the students nodded.

'Polyamorous relationships are "love" relationships, as I understand it,' said Em. She raised her mug, slugged back a mouthful of beer and slammed the mug down on the table. 'We will be a fucking sensation!'

She almost laughed as Jillian neatly added 'Fucking sensation' to her list.

'Of course it would be ideal to sell through our own website but we don't have time to get one up and running and generating subscribers. We'll have to start by selling the finished product to an established porn site. Thoughts?'

Tony, short, handsome and looking too young for college despite being 23, said, 'My folks don't talk to my uncle because he's in the porn business. I always liked him so I keep in touch, even do a few odd jobs for him over the summer. I know that he's always hungry for fresh faces, especially young ones.'

Emily grinned. She turned her hands palms up on the table. 'So there you go. If we can sell a set of three in each category we should be able to cover first semester for everyone. We'd probably still –'

For a moment she was drowned out by the cheers of her fellow students. Mugs were raised and emptied. She waited them out.

'We'd probably still have to keep shooting through the first semester, to pay for the second. Once we know what we're doing we'll be able to work faster. And our actors should have established at least a small fan base.'

'That's what worries me,' said Aileen. She was of

Asian descent and looked like the youngest in the group, though at 24 she was, in fact, the oldest.

Emily was surprised at how much it pleased her that this legal adult looked so young. God, she was already thinking like a porn producer. 'Go on.'

'I don't mind nudity. I'm even willing to do the "Love on the Run" stuff.' She shrugged. 'I like sex. But once I get pigeonholed as a porn actor, I'll never get a shot at becoming a movie star. Or, you know, not a star but –'

'A serious actress.'

Aileen nodded.

'Tell me –' Emily leaned forwards, catching and holding Aileen's almond-shaped dark eyes with her clear grey gaze '– what does an actor need to succeed?'

Aileen frowned. 'A good script, I guess. I don't know. Talent? Luck?'

Richard, the Tarantino freak, piped up, 'The Weinsteins! Harvey … "I want to party with you!"'

Trust Richard to waste a Weinstein sighting, even an imaginary one, by quoting a line from *Saving Silverman*. Em pushed on. 'Exactly. Except you don't need him, because you'll have me. I don't intend to produce porn for the rest of my life, either. My film company, our film company, will evolve into producing real movies and I pledge …' Emily picked up the Navajo bracelet and jumped up onto the table. She held the bracelet high. 'I pledge to the Gods of Film that I will take my actors and my crew with me, all the way to the top!'

As the group erupted in table-thumping, back-slapping, howling ebullience, Emily felt an intoxicating rush of adrenalin. It confused her for a moment but as the cheering erupted into a crowd chanting, 'Em-i-ly, Em-i-ly,' she recognised it for what it was ...

Power.

Chapter Seven

Emily pushed the fourth tedious tome aside and opened the fifth. Finding concrete examples of the 'trickle down effect' wasn't difficult, thanks to the Business Department's enormous library. It was just deadly boring. Still, she had to squeeze in some study time before exams or she'd be stuck with a pass in the major she wasn't supposed to have and a fail in the one she was. The words on the pages blurred. She'd added the much-coveted Saturday-night shift to her schedule at the restaurant. She needed money ... she had meetings scheduled ... she needed time ... but she wanted sleep ... her head drooped ...

A bright red file folder dropped on top of the fuzzy black and white pages. Emily's head jerked up with a start.

Marion and Jillian dragged sturdy chairs up to the oak table, oblivious to the noise they were making. Sure, the film programme had a library but not one full of students destined to be corporate suits. Emily shrugged in response to a chorus of hissed shushing noises.

'What's this?' Emily asked.

Marion flipped the file open. 'Dossiers on all our talent: names, ages, addresses, phone numbers, email addresses, measurements, who's in a couple and who isn't, sexual tastes, who'll do who for the good of the cause and who won't do who on camera.'

'Also proof of age, proof of negative STI status, real names and porno pseudonyms,' Jillian added. 'There are some things some of the girls don't want to do, for love or money, but surprisingly few. We're a horny bunch, it seems.'

Emily's eyebrows rose. 'Wow! That's great, you two. This'll make casting and selling much easier.'

'We've made copies for everyone who might need them,' Jillian said. 'Now, Marion sketched out a rough draft of the first script but –'

'I suck at dialogue,' said Marion. 'Sorry, kiddo. My heart's in sound.' She glanced around. 'Speaking of which, I've never been in a place with less ambient noise. It's like *Night of the Living Dead* in here. The original black and white version.' She shuddered.

'Kinda cool, though, the way the red folder stands out,' said Jillian. 'And, of course –' she stroked Marion's shining mop of curls '– your hair.'

Emily rubbed her eyes. 'I know,' she said. 'But I have to pass this course.'

Jillian pushed her chair back with a squeak. She started

massaging Emily's shoulders. 'Poor, producer gal. You work too hard.'

Only Emily seemed to notice the shocked faces of the other business students in the library and she didn't care. She knew she should. They were just as much her peers as the two lively girls who'd interrupted the solitude so necessary for serious study. But she didn't. Jillian's hands felt heavenly.

'What've you got so far, Marion?' she asked.

'In keeping with our theme of love,' said Marion, shuffling the papers in the red folder, 'you know Aileen, the mega-gorgeous Asian girl who looks underage?'

Emily nodded.

'I would so kill for her hair,' said Jillian.

'Harder,' Emily instructed Jillian.

Jillian kneaded Emily's neck with increased vigour.

Marion continued. 'She's keen to do Tony – the cute one with the porno uncle? Now Tony also looks younger than his years. Naturally, he's thrilled to be paired with Aileen and he did say his uncle's looking for fresh young faces so – *voilà*!'

Marion shoved the business books out of the way so she could place the head shots of Tony and Aileen side by side on the table. One of the books tumbled to the floor with a thump.

'Whoopsie!' Marion bent at the waist to pick it up. She threw in a wiggle before she heaved the tome to the table.

Emily giggled. She felt giddy, almost drunk. For a moment, she couldn't place the sensation but it dawned on her, as if from a dream or another lifetime, that this was called 'fun'.

'Aileen lives in the dorm,' said Jillian. She rubbed her thumbs in the spaces between Emily's vertebrae.

Emily moaned. That got the attention of anyone who wasn't already glaring (the women) or staring (the men) at her table. She closed her eyes. *Take a flying fuck at the moon.*

'So we can't really shoot in her room. But I picked up a bolt of pink satin for pennies at the Hadassah Bazaar on the weekend, so I can make any bedroom, well, except the ones that are painted black or something, look like a girl's room in her parents' home.'

'We'll use my place,' said Emily. 'It'll be more private.'

'Perf!' Marion exclaimed. She placed a disc on the table. 'Like I said, the story's there, such as it is, but the dialogue is shit.'

Reluctantly, Emily opened her eyes. She blinked rapidly.

'You need sleep,' scolded Jillian.

'Later,' said Emily. She straightened her back. 'Marion, tell Luke we shoot in three days. He'll have the script by noon tomorrow. He needs to assemble his crew and at least run through the script with the cast. This is not an improvisational piece. That's key to the project.'

She reassembled the red folder as she spoke.

'I want you to be his first assistant director.' She avoided Marion's eyes and pretended she didn't hear the curvaceous girl's surprised gasp. At the moment, whatever past Marion and Luke did or did not have was of no interest. Emily was damn sure Marion was her best choice for the job.

'Jillian, get his key to my place. I'll be out by six a.m. so you can start dressing the set any time after that. I'm writing an exam on Thursday and then working the dinner shift so I won't be sticking my producer-face in on the shoot, much as I might like to. Got that?'

Jillian nodded.

Emily flipped her laptop open and inserted Marion's disc. She looked up and feigned surprise that the two women were still there. 'So? Any questions?'

They shook their heads.

'Scram. I've got a script to write.'

'Yes, ma'am,' squeaked Jillian.

They fled the library.

Emily flashed her fellow Business students a brilliant smile. As they bent their heads to their studies, she heard one woman grumble about 'the nerve of some people'.

Oh, baby, you ain't seen nothin' yet.

Emily opened Movie Magic and set her fingers to the keys.

Chapter Eight

Six days later, Luke brought a disc with their finished product on it to Emily's apartment. Knotted inside with fearful anticipation, Emily sat on her couch and told Luke, 'Do it!'

His trembling fingers fed the disc to her DVD player. 'Here's what we did with your script, Em. I hope you like it.'

The name of the short film, *Young Love*, appeared on the screen, followed by the plain name – they didn't have a logo yet – of their almost born company.

A NAKED AND IN LOVE PRODUCTION

Emily clutched at Luke's thigh. He covered her hand with his own. On the screen ...

Aileen, dressed in loafers, thin OTK white socks, a short pleated skirt, white shirt and striped tie, hair in bunches, entered her bedroom, followed by Tony in jeans and a tight white T-shirt. Aileen had turned out to be a whiz with make-up. Somehow, she'd made him look even younger than he usually did. They let book bags thump to the floor.

'You sure my coming over is OK with your folks?' he asked.

'I told you, baby, they're away for the weekend, so we can "study" as late as we like, right?' She threw herself backwards onto the bed. The motion flipped her short skirt high enough to expose a plump triangle nestled in her plain white cotton panties.

'It took four takes to get her skirt to fall that way,' Luke told Emily.

'Was it worth it?'

'Tony says there are lots of guys into "up-skirt". See the way the cotton moulds into the crease of her pubes? That's called a "camel toe", also very popular.'

'So who "moulded" it?'

'Not me, honest. She did it herself.'

'Maybe I better come to the next shoot, just to keep an eye on you.'

'You'd be welcome, really, but you know you can trust me, Em.'

Emily grinned. 'I know, and you don't want your executive producer watching over your shoulder. No directors do.'

Luke nibbled her ear. 'They would if the producer was you.'

'Sssh.'

On the screen, Tony was sitting next to Aileen and leaning over her. Her shirt had pulled out of the waistband of her skirt, exposing a thin strip of tummy. He bent lower, lips pursed as if to kiss the tantalising ribbon of skin, but pulled back as if uncertain.

'Is it OK if I kiss you?' he asked Aileen.

'You've kissed me before.'

'I know, but ...'

She pulled his face to hers and brushed her lips over his.

'Oh, sweetheart,' he moaned. 'I do love you.'

She answered by parting her lips and running her tongue across his.

'Did I write him as being a bit too slow, do you think?' Emily asked.

'Guys like to be seduced.'

'I never had to seduce you,' Emily said.

'With us it was mutual.'

Emily moved her hand from his thigh to his crotch. 'Mutual is good.'

The couple in the video were kissing passionately by then but their lips weren't pressed together so that the viewer could see their tongues writhe together.

'Oh good!' Emily said. 'You managed to show their tongues the way I asked.'

'I shot what you wrote, Emily, as much as possible.'

'That deserves to be rewarded.'

'Rewarded?'

She tugged the tab of his zipper down.

'Oh – *rewarded*.'

'Watch the movie,' she told him.

'You too.'

'I don't watch with my hands.' The fingers of her right hand slipped into his fly. Her other hand worked on his belt buckle. 'You know, Luke, watching my words come to life on the screen is a big turn-on for me.'

'Me too. Knowing that this is all out of your imagination is like you're fucking me with your head.'

'Head? Did you say "head"?'

'You know what I mean, but now that you mention it ...'

'That I can't do and watch the screen at the same time. How about this?' She pulled his fever-hot cock out of his jeans.

'Take it slow, OK? I don't want to ...'

'It's called "premature ejaculation".'

'I know that, Em. It's never been a problem of mine.'

'True. But I feel like I could come any minute, too.'

The couple on the screen were still kissing passionately but now Tony was gently caressing that tantalising strip of bare skin between Aileen's skirt and her shirt.

'Tony knows to take his time,' Emily observed.

'Under my direction,' Luke reminded her.

'Of course, Lukey. And following my script.'

'Of course.'

Tony's finger hooked under Aileen's waistband and stroked from side to side, each time pushing her skirt a little lower. She co-operated by sucking her tummy in. Without their lips parting, the on-screen lovers worked Aileen's skirt down to her knees. She kicked it off. Tony's hand hovered above the girl's mound as if uncertain. As if making its mind up, it moved higher, to work on the buttons of her shirt. When it was parted and spread, he lifted his head. He asked, 'Have you ...? I mean, are you ...?'

'A virgin?' Aileen asked. She tugged her tie from around her neck. 'Have I ...' She paused as if searching for a word. Her '*fucked* anyone?' was emphatic, daring him to object to her choice of words. 'Yes, I have. Twice. Is that a problem?'

'No, no, not at all. It's just ...'

'You haven't?' Her voice almost squeaked.

He shook his head.

'Oh!' She pulled his face down to her chest. 'You poor boy. I just assumed ...'

They lay there for a long awkward moment.

'If I don't do it right ...' Tony started.

'Don't be silly. You'll be great – and I'll be fucking a virgin!'

'Is that good?'

'It's ... an honour, I think. I'll be very proud to be your first.'

'Really?'

'You bet. Lift your head.'

He did so. Aileen unhooked her delicate little cotton bra from between her breasts and tugged it away. She cupped her breasts and offered them to him. 'Start here, please, sweetheart. Drive me crazy.'

'I'm not sure how.'

'Just the thought is getting me hot, so I promise you'll have no problems. You're a great kisser. You're young and good-looking and very sweet. You're enough to get any girl steamed up.'

'Really?'

'Really.'

'You're so beautiful,' he told her.

'You like my tits?'

'Love them.'

'Make my nipples hard then.'

'How – I mean, I know how. I've played with girls' tits before but how *exactly* do you want me to do it?'

'The dialogue is working well, don't you think?' Emily asked Luke.

'That's where we'll score,' Luke said. 'Most pornos have lousy dialogue, if any. The way you've written this, these are real people, not just bodies. They're learning about each other, exploring each other's wants and needs. There's an underlying tension that –'

Emily gave his shaft a long slow stroke that put an

abrupt end to his diatribe. 'Thank you, Mr Director. Would you pause the movie, please?'

'Huh?'

Emily jumped up and returned with a couple of Cokes and a bowl of ice.

'You want to last for the whole movie? No "premature ejaculation"?'

'Yes, but …?'

Emily dipped her hand into ice water before taking hold of his cock again. 'This should help.'

'Brrr.'

'No?'

'Yes. Yes-yes, not yes-no.'

'I think I see steam rising.'

Luke looked down at himself.

'Joking, silly!' Emily planted a big kiss on his lips.

He hit 'play'.

On screen, Aileen told Tony, 'I guess it isn't fair for boys, is it? We girls expect you to know how we like to be touched but we don't even tell you if you're doing good or bad. You're supposed to guess. Sit up.' She followed to an upright position and tugged his shirt off over his head before pushing him down again, this time with her leaning over him. 'This is what *I* like. Not all girls are the same.'

She wet a fingertip and smoothed it over the tip of his nipple. 'How's that feel?'

Tony shrugged. 'Nothing, really. I guess boys' nipples are different from girls'.'

'Shame. You miss a lot then. OK, just take this as a demonstration.' She continued making little circles over his nipple as she leaned her head down towards his. 'But don't forget the kissing.' Her tongue slipped into his mouth. Between sucking his tongue and exploring his mouth she showed him how to finger her nipples, gently and with wet fingertips, brushing, rolling, building up to demanding little pinches. Tony reciprocated, copying her actions. Aileen began to arch and writhe above him.

'That's so good,' she panted into his mouth. 'Now use your mouth, please. Lick? Suck? Nibble?'

Tony acted the eager pupil well, though Emily was sure that the enthusiasm he showed was genuine. Judging by her own reactions to the script she'd written, her idea of a slightly more experienced girl teaching a virgin boy how to screw was working.

Aileen said, 'Suck hard, very hard. My nip is excited now so you won't hurt it unless you bite it, but don't, OK?'

'OK.' Tony sucked, drawing a nipple and half a breast into his mouth.

'Yes!' Aileen said. 'Look at it. See what you've done to me?'

The boy inspected Aileen's angrily engorged spike. 'It didn't hurt?'

64

'Only in a good way. Take your jeans off now, please. And your underwear. I want your cock out where I can see it.'

'Right now, if you touch it, it'll explode.'

'No it won't, but I don't need to touch it yet anyway. I want to see what you caressing me does to it. A cock can't pay a fake compliment. Your cock will tell me exactly how much you like me.'

Tony stood up and stripped bare. 'But pussies can lie?'

'Some, but when they get wet inside, that's pretty sincere.'

He joined her on the bed. 'Is yours wet inside?'

'Very. Wet, hot and needy.'

Tony groaned with lust.

'You've touched a girl inside before, with your fingers?'

He nodded.

'But not with your cock?'

He shook his head.

'You will today, I promise. Be patient and I'll make it all worthwhile.'

He mumbled something incoherent.

Aileen giggled. 'I love making you ache for it.'

'Bitch!'

'Yeah! Suffer, lover!' She pushed him flat and leaned over him to look down on his crotch. 'From the look of that handsome cock, you must really like me, a lot.'

'I do!' he moaned. 'Honest, I do.'

'Enough to be very patient?'

'I *am* being patient, aren't I?'

Aileen blew gently on the wet head of his cock. He jerked, halfway sitting up before subsiding with yet another tormented groan.

'We've got two whole days,' she promised, and lay back. 'Look at what I'm doing.'

He sat up.

Aileen traced the crease in her panties' 'camel toe' with a pointed nail. 'See the little bump at the top?'

'Your clit, right?'

'Good boy. Now watch.' Her nail scratched through the cotton, very lightly, at the head of her clit. 'This feels good,' she told him. 'Kiss me some more and suck on my nipples, but at the same time, scratch me like I'm doing. Pretty soon, I won't be able to bear it any more, and then – well, you'll see what happens then.'

Tony's lips travelled from Aileen's mouth, to nipple, to nipple, gradually becoming more confident and masterful. The muscles in Aileen's flat tummy clenched and relaxed, slowly but becoming faster. Her legs stretched out off the end of the bed, toes pointed. She began to pant.

Tony kept tantalising her body with obvious relish.

In her living room, Emily dipped her hand back into the ice water and took a fresh grip on Luke's shaft.

Luke asked, 'Is that how you'd like me to do you, Em?'

'You do me just fine, but yes, being driven crazy is

always nice for me. Isn't it for you?' She gave him a slow stroke.

He sucked air. 'The longer, the better.'

On screen, Aileen was twitching. The long muscles in her slender thighs began to quiver. When Tony nibbled on her nipples, she bit her lower lip. Her head tossed from side to side, whipping the bed with her bunches. Her legs bent and drew up until her bottom came off the bed. Her eyes opened in a blind stare. 'Fuck!' burst from her lips. 'You fucking bastard! You've. Made. Me. Come!'

Tony's face fell.

Aileen rolled into a ball and rocked. The boy looked as if he didn't know what to do, whether to feel proud or guilty.

Aileen sat up and pushed Tony onto his back. 'Don't worry.' She was panting. 'I don't just come once. That was a warm-up.' She skinned out of her panties and tossed them aside. 'You want to fuck me now?'

He nodded, speechless.

She threw a leg across his body. Glaring down at him, she told him, 'Well, you aren't going to. You know why?'

His 'No,' was pathetic.

'Because I am going to fuck you!'

Aileen hitched up, took Tony's cock in her hand and came down on it, hard and fast. 'Lie still!' she ordered.

He nodded.

Aileen bucked and ground, leaned forwards and back,

rocked and jerked, making it very obvious that she was seeking her own pleasure, not his. 'Don't come,' she ordered. 'You can twist my nipples, but don't come.'

Her fists pounded the bed to either side of Tony's head. 'I'm crazy for your cock,' she told him. 'I want you to come in my mouth. Can you hold it till then?'

He nodded, though he looked unsure.

'Hold my shoulders and pull me down!'

He obeyed. She ground down harder and tighter, face distorted with lust.

'Is that your direction?' Emily asked Luke. 'If so, you're good, and she's an excellent actress.'

'Some of each, I think. That was the first time I saw Aileen fuck, remember. I've got no other occasions to compare it to.'

'She seems to enjoy the work.'

'I think that knowing she was actually starring in a movie helped.'

'A natural,' Emily agreed. 'Terrific close-ups too, Luke.'

On the screen, Aileen screamed out another orgasm and seemed to shrink into herself for a second before she recovered and dismounted Tony's straining erection.

'Good cock,' she praised. 'Come now. Give me all your nice hot cream.'

Her mouth covered Tony's cock. Aileen's cheeks hollowed.

Tony burst out, 'I can't hold back any longer!'

Aileen nodded. Her lips slid from his base off the tip of his cock. She gave his shaft little licks as she reassured him. 'That's OK. We've got an entire weekend. There's lots of time and lots of things for us to try – everything either of us wants.' Her head lowered as she took all of him in her mouth; her lips dragged along the thin, tight skin as she pulled back. Her hand rubbed the dome of Tony's cock on the flat of her tongue.

'You didn't forget the "money shot" then,' Emily said.

'No way.'

Tony climaxed, one thick jet directly into Aileen's mouth, three lesser ones onto her tongue.

She swallowed most of it, but allowed a little to dribble down her chin. 'Was that good for you?' Aileen asked Tony.

'Wow!'

'While we take a break, you can think about all the nasty things you'd like to do to me,' Aileen said.

'And then?'

'And then we'll do them.' She turned to face the camera and gave it a big wink.

'What was that last bit?' Emily asked Luke.

'Even before it was edited, I was sure we had something hot going on so I added that wink as a way to promise the audience that there'd be more. What do you think?'

'I like it. We'll shoot a trilogy with just those two, on

the same set. I'll move out if I have to. Tony and Aileen have chemistry.'

'The catalyst was your script, Emily.'

'Thanks. You're right. I could write another for those two, easy as anything. I'm starting to get ideas right now.' Her grip on his shaft tightened.

'What ideas?'

'How about I show you instead of tell you. That's what the movies are all about, right?'

'Right. Want me to get the camera? You know, just for us. Not to sell.'

'Of course not.' Emily meant that but at the same time Aileen had set the bar very high. Emily couldn't help but wonder if she'd be able to turn in a sexier performance. She could certainly try.

Chapter Nine

'Quiet on the set!'

Even though they'd shot for most of the day and taken only a fifteen-minute break, the words were music to Luke's ears.

'NAIL Productions Limited,' yelled Jillian. '*Sweet Cheeks*, Scene Two, Take One!' She snapped the clapperboard.

'Rolling,' said Jimmy, the director of photography. The camera was focused on the closed door to Emily's bedroom.

Luke paused for a moment. Jillian had done an amazing job of transforming Emily's living room into the main room of a bridal suite. A wine bucket with crushed ice nestling a sparkling water-filled Dom Perignon bottle sat on the pink satin tablecloth that covered Em's thrift-store kitchen table. The love seat was covered with a soft 'suede' throw. Two champagne flutes (one on its side) and a large, torn banner that proclaimed 'HAPPY

HONEYMOON' pretty much set the scene. The wedding dress, which Gary had only gotten half-off Kara before fucking her on the floor (a difficult scene that had taken much more time than Luke had anticipated but which he'd filmed with so many close-ups it was a wonder the money shot hadn't hit the camera lens) lay in a crinolined heap of fluff and sequins in front of the love seat. It'd been worth the time, but it meant there'd been literally no rehearsal time for Scene Two and he hoped to get the rest of the piece in the can without a lot of reshoots.

Reshoots. He wondered how many Gary had in him. So far, the guy seemed to be up to the job of fucking his exotic and gorgeous girlfriend twenty-four-seven.

Luke had agreed with Emily and taken a gamble, having Gary chase his almost naked 'bride' into the bedroom at the end of the first scene. They hoped it would pique the interest of the viewer. *What the hell is going on in the bedroom that we don't get to see? What kind of porn is this?*Now it was time to reward that audience for its nanosecond of faith with a scorching finale.

Marion, his first assistant director, caught his eye. She gave him an imperceptible nod of encouragement.

'Action!' yelled Luke.

The bedroom door burst open and Kara charged into the room, wearing the white satin bustière that laced up the back and white stay-ups (one with a ladder she'd complained of in Scene One) and stilettos she'd had on at the end of the scene. Her chest and face were freshly fucked pink in a pleasant contrast to virginal white. Her breasts bounced in their twin satin cradles and her dark, hard nipples played peek-a-boo with the viewer as she raced around the room.

'No!' she screamed.

Gary charged after her, buck-naked. He was hirsute (albeit with a clean-shaven face); from chest to ankles he was dark with black hair. His pubes and underarms were thick with it. He carried a bottle of lube and, as he pursued his prey, he pumped some into his other hand and fisted it onto his rigid cock.

Luke flashed Marion a peace sign. She was already positioned beside the second cameraman and now she tapped his shoulder.

While Jimmy, the operator of camera one as well as D.P., continued to shoot the full scene, Paul's camera two followed the cock's progress, zoomed in at the prear-ranged mark just as Gary's cock paused, then panned slowly back to resume its pursuit of the bride.

This was their first two-camera shoot and everyone was pretty pumped up about it. Luke wanted Gary's hard-on, as it zeroed in on Kara like a heat-seeking missile, shot up close and real personal. It seemed he was getting what he wanted.

'You promised, Mrs Bottomsby.'

'I'm not ready,' pleaded Kara. She collapsed in the

middle of her oh-so-recently abandoned wedding gown. 'I'm too scared.'

'I'll make you ready, baby, don't worry. And don't be scared. You're gonna love this.'

Gary pounced on Kara. He kissed her long and hard. She visibly relaxed. 'I love you, Mr Bottomsby.'

'I love you, too,' he said. 'Now assume the position!'

Kara burst into tears. She grasped the head of the hidden zipper in the front of her bustière and in a moment the lingerie was unzipped and discarded, the lacing up the back as tight as ever.

The crew looked as one to their leader. Even Marion, who'd performed the unsung, essential duties of First A.D. with such finesse Luke had begun to wonder how he'd ever directed without her, goggled at him.

He made a short, circular motion with his index finger. *Keep rolling.* They hadn't had a lot of time for rehearsal but he was one hundred per cent certain his leading lady was not in real distress.

Gary gave Kara a sharp smack on each cheek of her bum. 'Spread 'em baby, or I'll spread 'em for you.'

Make that ninety per cent.

Kara sniffled and knelt up nicely, her elbows on the brushed fake suede of the sofa, her knees and thighs surrounded by netting and crepe. The look she gave Gary, over her shoulder, was wide-eyed and reproachful.

'Please, husband … don't hurt me.'

Gary grinned. He licked his lips. He parted the cheeks of her ass with his hands, exposing Kara's pink asshole. He sat back, as if admiring it, giving camera two ample time to zoom in and hold on a tight close-up of her tight hole.

Luke nodded, Marion tapped, and camera two zoomed in.

'Aww, baby, you know you can trust me,' said Gary. He leaned in, teasing her hole with the tip of his tongue. 'Doesn't that feel just like a ... like a rose petal, caressing your pretty little virgin hole, all soft and sweet?'

'Ye– yes.'

'Mm ... gorgeous ... every inch of you is so fucking gorgeous I feel ... one minute I feel like I could ... mm ... I could lavish you with little kisses all day ...'

Kara arched her back a little, presenting her bottom as Mrs Vixen might present hers to Mr Fox. Her head tilted back, as if his low, cooing praise was, like his tongue, imparting such a delicate sense that she needed to lean in a little to catch it.

'... and the next –' Gary fisted another dollop of lube onto his dick '– the next I want to roar with pride!' He rolled back onto his heels, lifted an inch and jammed his cock to its hilt up Kara's ass.

Kara screamed.

Gary roared.

Luke stepped back. Hadn't Kara agreed to star in a

porn shoot as long as it wasn't 'too kinky'? This stuff was so *not* in the script. He pointed at his ear. Marion tapped the soundman on his back. He nodded. She nodded.

Gary pulled almost all the way out.

Tears rolled down Kara's cheeks. 'Honey, it hurts, it hurts.'

'Only for a minute, sweetcheeks,' Gary said. 'Trust me, baby.'

'I do.'

'There's my girl. I do. Remember what you promised, now. I promise to love.' He buried his cock in her ass in another smooth, hard stroke. This time his body dropped forwards, too, so that his chest was against her back and his arms and hands on either side of hers, keeping her in place.

'Honour.'

Kara's head dropped a little.

His mouth pressed up close to her ear.

'And *obey*.'

Her head shuddered in three little nods. Her tears dripped straight down onto the brushed suede, staining it.

Luke motioned to Marion to let Paul, on camera two, know it was time to pull back a little, staying tight on the couple. It was nuts to shoot like this, one long take, but he was goddamned if he'd call 'Cut.' Camera one was getting the full picture. They could get all the pick-ups and cutaways they'd need, later, if Kara was really OK but if that poor chick was being forced by her boyfriend to take it up the ass for the cameras, he'd never get these shots unless he got them now. Which was one of the worst things he'd ever thought in his life, but he couldn't dwell on that now.

Kara's ass began to rotate.

Gary whispered, 'You're so brave.'

She mewled. Her hips rolled in tight little circles.

Gary leaned hard on his left arm and raised his right hand to tuck her damp hair behind her ear. 'My brave, beautiful woman.'

Camera two was right there to shoot her wet face and messed up make-up and her pendant breasts, heaving with each shuddering breath she took.

'Uh-huh,' Kara muttered.

Camera one swivelled to capture Gary's ass as his pace increased. His balls slapped Kara's inner thighs with each stroke. Gary was humping her now. The fingers of his right hand pinched each of her nipples, hard, before dropping to her splayed lower lips to find and torture her clit.

Kara's mutterings and mewlings grew in volume until they matched Gary's roar in volume and intent.

'Fuck my ass, then, if it's so fucking important to you. Fuck me till you kill me, I don't care. You're my fucking husband, you pervert, you fucking animal!'

That's it! Exactly what Emily and Luke wanted. Lovers, fucking like dogs. *Christ!*

Luke glanced at his crew. *Oh Gods of Film, please let them be getting all this.*

'Yeah?' Gary pounded into her. His left hand gripped the back of the sofa while his right continued torturing her clit. 'You like it like this, baby?'

His hips drew back, slammed forwards. Again. Again. 'Answer me, you slut, or I'll stop right now.'

'Don't stop! Please! Don't stop.'

'I told you I wasn't going to make you do something you don't want, sweetheart. So, you want it?'

Again Kara's head shuddered in a miniature nod.

Gary slowed. He withdrew his cock until all but the tip was free of her. 'I can't hear you, sweetheart.'

'I fucking love it! I love it when you fuck me up the ass. OK?'

'OK!'

Gary pummelled Kara's stretched asshole until her moans, protests and demands fused into one long, loud, unintelligible groan.

'So –' Gary panted between words '– close.'

His pace slowed.

Fuck. Don't let him run out of steam now. Luke shot Marion a helpless look. Was he as red-faced as she was? He nodded.

Marion tapped Paul on his shoulder.

Camera two moved in for the money shot.

Kara threw her head back. 'Yes! Yes! Fuck!'

Gary slowed a little more, thrusting at an even, medium pace.

Kara ground her ass against his crotch at the end of each stroke. She pounded the sofa with her fists. Tears flowed. Her mouth hung open, loose and wet, as her shrieks dropped to moans and her moans to little peeps of pleasure.

'OK, baby?' Gary stroked her back.

Kara nodded.

'OK, baby!' Gary thrust hard and fast, three times, then gripped her hips with both hands and roared.

Money shot, money shot …

Gary jerked his cock from Kara's ass and slapped it onto her back where it pulsed, spewing cream with each one.

'I … I love you, Mrs Bottomsby,' he said.

His cock slid off her back and drooped between his legs. He pressed his chest to her back. He licked the sweat from the right side of her neck.

Kara turned her head. 'I love you too, Mr Bottomsby,' she said.

They kissed.

And kissed.

And kissed.

'Cut,' said Luke.

The cameras stopped filming; the sound stopped rolling.

Kara and Gary stopped kissing.

Marion stepped forwards. 'Kara, are you ... are you OK?'

Kara frowned.

'Yeah,' said Luke. 'Because you did say you didn't want to do anything too kinky. So, I mean, I know you knew what the script was about but if you weren't comfortable I need you to let me know right now and I'll make sure it never happens again.'

Kara and Gary collapsed on the sullied wedding dress, laughing like idiots.

Kara managed to sputter, 'Luke, honey, anal sex doesn't count as kinky.' She wiped her face on Gary's chest hair. 'Gary and I fuck like that all the time!'

Chapter Ten

Emily remained standing on the bus while Luke and Tony took seats. It wasn't a case of them not offering her a free seat. Em was wearing a white summer power suit made of one hundred per cent linen, a 'stand-up' suit. She'd sit when they got to the meeting. She glanced down at her platform peep-toe sandals. There was that toe cleavage Luke had taught her about. Her legs were white; she hadn't been willing to risk a fake tan and lounging in the sun was not on the cards for this particular summer. Still, pale though they may be, they were long and her ankles were, or so she'd been told, delicate. A light pink cami, in keeping with the season's mania for pastels, completed her look. She wore very little make-up. It was the paradox of sexy and lovely that she wanted to sell so she'd decided to start making the point the moment she entered the meeting.

Essentially, it was vital that Tony's uncle, Vito Manero, buy their set of six short porn movies. Em could only hope Tony really was on their side and hadn't told his uncle how desperately the fledgling porn company needed money. They could shoot as many sexy little movies as they wanted and it would do them no good without distribution.

It was the last Friday in July. Only Luke remained in school, learning how to shoot sixty-second commercials and sports events during the day and directing NAIL short porn flicks at night.

A few of the cast and crew had left when the school year ended, but Luke and his roommates had stayed in their big house close to the campus. They always did, since they had to pay rent on their rooms during the summer months anyway, or lose them. This summer, however, most of them worked full-time for NAIL, instead of finding secure jobs. Even those who'd left had been asked to return on 1st August for a blitz of production before the first semester of their final year commenced. So everyone involved with NAIL was making a leap of faith and Emily was fully, achingly aware of the risk.

Emily waitressed at Bailey's six nights a week. She worked on NAIL six days a week. True to his word, Blaine had handed Emily a shell company his father had given him and Emily had completed the tedious work of turning it into a film production company. Naked And In Love Productions Limited still needed a proper logo, but the company was established and registered.

On Sundays, she and Luke were supposed to forget about everything and spend the day together, but it was getting more and more difficult to turn it off and she knew Luke felt the same.

Sometimes they simply slept all day and shared a simple dinner. Other times they actually managed to make love. No matter how hard Em laid down the law, her apartment was always a disaster so part of the day had to be spent doing housework, which she, in particular, resented. Bad enough she only had three uniforms for a six night a week gig, making laundry and ironing a must. She didn't think she should have to mop up after her crew like a janitor. However, since most of them were receiving what amounted to an allowance for their constant hard work, none seemed willing to don the janitor's cap, either.

Most Sundays, if they had time, Luke and Em went for a walk and talked business. It couldn't be helped. Their future and the futures of their friends weighed heavily on them both.

Tony stood. Emily picked up her soft leather brief-case and she and Luke followed him off the bus. They walked in silence. It was a newly developed area, mainly industrial strip plazas, monotonous red brick. The one they wanted was mainly two storey, with five-storey 'one tenant' buildings at each corner. Manero Triple X Adult Film Distribution was one of them. Five floors in a new plaza? Business had to be good.

They entered, single file, Emily and her briefcase, which contained six half-hour NAIL Productions Ltd films of varying degrees of quality, in the middle.

Why did she feel like a criminal? There was nothing illegal going on here. Even the revolting pseudo-rape anal sex tape was a performance by consenting adults.

She dredged up the memory of an interview Sir Laurence Olivier had done. He and the series he'd done the interview for were old but his words rang as true as ever. In answer to a complicated question by the understandably nervous young interviewer, Sir Larry had leaned back and replied, in that marvellous drawl he often employed for emphasis, 'It's called *acting*, dear boy.'

They were greeted by a receptionist with a Brooklyn accent. Right. Tony had mentioned her. Naturally, Manero had an office in New York and where he went his executive assistant went with him.

'Welcome to Manero Triple X Adult Film Distribution,' said the woman, largely through her perfect nose. *Nose job*. Christ. Emily was driving herself insane. She'd had a nose job, too. Although hers was, at least in part, because of a deviated septum …

The shit stops here.

With Olivier's words ringing in her ears, she tilted up her chin, squared her shoulders, and became Ms Emily Forrester, Executive Producer of NAIL.

'Good afternoon –' she glanced at the name plate on

the woman's desk, although Tony had already told her what it was '– Melody. We're from NAIL Productions Limited. Emily Forrester and Luke Rayellton. I think you already know –'

'Tony, my baby!' Melody leaped to her feet. Her bosom was magnificent, but not overtly displayed. Emily decided not to hold it against her. As far as she could tell, those tits were the real thing. Melody tottered in stilettos and a pencil skirt around her desk to capture Tony in an effusive embrace that made Bobby's Brazilian greeting seem standoffish in comparison.

Tony grinned at Emily and Luke over Melody's shoulder. His eyebrows lifted as if to say, *What can I do but accept it?*

After what seemed an appropriate amount of time had passed, Emily cleared her throat. 'We have an appointment with Mr Manero for three o'clock?'

'Right. Right!' Melody released Tony. He straightened himself and took a deep breath, with the grin of a village idiot plastered on his face.

'Walk this way,' said Melody. She opened a door and minced through it.

Tony did the same, right down to the mince.

Luke grinned.

'Don't think I don't know what your doin', Tony,' said Melody. 'You're not so big I can't put you over my knee.'

'Promises, promises.' Tony sighed.

Luke laughed.

Emily was already looking past them, at the man behind the desk; the man who held all of their futures in his hands.

Make this happen.

She kept her eyes locked on Vito Manero while Melody presented him with his nephew and 'friends'.

Manero gave Tony a hug and Luke a handshake but his eyes were locked on Emily's, too.

'Emily Forrester, Executive Producer of Naked And In Love Productions Limited.'

'Vito Manero of Manero Triple X Adult Film Distribution. Everybody, take a seat!'

They did, with Emily furthest to the right, putting her as close to the man in the power seat as possible. She flipped open the top of her case and crossed her ankles. Mr Manero was nothing like she'd expected. She tried to avoid stereotyping but, in his case, she'd failed. He sold porn, for goodness' sake! He had no business having freshly coifed iron-grey hair, aquiline features and a broad-shouldered trim body. He wasn't even wearing pastel polyester, as she'd imagined. His Armani suit was charcoal barathea and his Sulka tie matched, but with narrow stripes of dove grey.

After declining coffee and tea and accepting bottled water, the three representatives of the neophyte film company received a short, solid education in the business of porn production.

When he stressed 'legality', Emily placed the NAIL Productions Ltd information on his desk. When he stressed 'clean and adult' actors she placed the sheaf of head shots and accompanying information of her cast beside the paperwork on NAIL.

So far, so good.

Once Melody delivered the bottled water and the three students had cracked them open (with only Tony spilling onto his cords) Manero put his hands on his desk, palms up, and said, 'So, what can we do for each other, business-wise?'

Emily began with their most romantic short, the third and last in the series starring Tony and Aileen. She flipped through the discs in her briefcase until she found *Young Love, III*. In it, Tony, now an accomplished lover, brings his demanding but unfaithful girlfriend, Aileen, to a climax so stupendous that she declares her fidelity for evermore.

She rose, smoothing her linen skirt, and walked to the DVD player. If there was a wiggle to her walk that wasn't always there, well, her business shoes had platform heels and Manero's floors were polished to a gloss. She could hardly afford to fall on her face now, could she?

She bent, turned on the TV and DVD player, inserted the disc, and returned to her seat with the remote in hand. She tossed it into Luke's lap and leaned forwards, palms flat, onto Manero's desk. She and Manero were face to face.

'Let's see,' she cooed. She jerked her head at Luke. He hit the remote.

Emily took a slug of water from her bottle and wiped the back of her hand across her mouth. *Too much?*

Manero seemed mesmerised.

Em took her seat and turned her eyes to the monitor. She'd made the wrong choice, obviously, but it was too late to change her mind. The *Young Love* trilogy was so damned romantic, a celebration of Eros. This man's mind had to be saturated with porn. He'd hate it, for sure, because it was so 'vanilla'. She should have started with something powerful, like the honeymoon anal-fuck film.

Vito was intent on the screen, deadpan. Being polite, of course. Watching the entire movie because his nephew was involved.

She crossed her legs, letting her skirt ride up her thighs. As she watched, she licked her lips from time to time and tilted her water bottle to her mouth, wriggled in her seat and in general gave Manero such a show she'd be damned if he wasn't as hard as the stupid miniature cannon that squatted on his desk. *Ready, set, fire, Manero.* As the piece grew to a close, with the couple declaring their love all over again, at a feverish pitch, she allowed a tear to slide down the side of her cheek. As if embarrassed, she swiped it away, making sure Manero caught all of it.

Whore.

Emily gave him her most angelic smile. Her grey eyes

were misted with emotion. She tucked a flyaway strand of honey-coloured hair behind her ear. 'Well, sir, what do you think of romance and X-rated sex now?'

'You're good,' he said. 'Fuck.' Manero wiped his face from the top of his forehead to the bottom of his chin. 'Fuck me.

'Your timing is perfect,' he told them. 'You know, the readership of sex books used to be seventy per cent male, thirty per cent female. Then the internet happened. Guys like me, we churned out every sort of erotic movie a man could dream of and men, being more visual than women, stopped reading and started watching. Now, the per cents are reversed when it comes to reading porn. It's seventy per cent female, thirty per cent male. Fewer women watch porn movies, though they love sexy-romantic ones. They like "happily ever after" to mean more than a money shot.'

Luke and Emily exchanged glances. They'd pretty much worked all this out for themselves but they sure weren't going to interrupt Vito's lecture.

'I've been thinking for some time, thirty per cent of our potential market isn't being serviced. I wondered how we could combine good raw sex with romance and make it work for both male and female audiences. You'd think it'd be easy, but no one has done it before. You know why?'

All three shook their heads.

'One, most porn isn't written by writers. It's made up as it's shot. Two, in the main, porn stars can't act. They can't even deliver dialogue, and I don't mean just when their mouths are full of cock.'

Emily grinned to show that she wasn't offended by his language. If they were going to do business, in this business, cocks and pussies were merchandise that would be discussed.

'Somehow,' he said, 'you've managed to create at least token plots, and you've added the emotional content that women viewers will go ape over, I guarantee it. If you can keep this quality up, I'll buy all you can make.' He pulled a pad over and wrote on it before pushing it to Emily. 'How does this grab you?'

When she read the number on the pad, she coughed to cover up her gasp. 'I think we can work with that, Mr Manero.'

'Call me Vito.'

'Vito, then.'

'Great. Listen, your cast – the kids look clean, are clean. Make sure they stay that way.'

'Yes, sir. Everyone will continue to be tested once a month.'

Vito nodded. 'And no messy stuff, know what I mean? I sell legal porn, for entertainment purposes. You want to make the big bucks, skirt the law, take your chances – don't bring that crap to me.'

'I feel exactly the same way.' Emily leaned forwards and pounded his desk with her fist for emphasis. 'NAIL wants our product to be as much fun for the talent to make as it is for the viewer to watch.'

'So.' Vito extended his hand. 'Welcome to the porn industry.'

Emily grasped his hand. 'Thank you, Vito.'

They shook on it.

Tony and Luke exchanged excited looks but stayed in their seats. It was Emily who, overcome with delight, wriggled to her feet. 'We've got so much more to show you.'

'I'm sure you do,' Vito drawled, shaking his head. 'But I've seen enough for now. Leave the rest of them with Melody. I'll be in touch.'

On the bus ride home, Tony couldn't stop yammering about how Emily had played his uncle 'like a pro'.

She preferred to think he meant professional filmmaker and didn't ask for a definition.

Luke stared out the window.

Emily, using her briefcase balanced on her knees as a desk, a contract and a calculator on top, kept tapping keys and staring at the figures.

'A good day's work,' she said. She'd already said it a couple of times but she didn't know what else to say or do. So she just kept calculating and recalculating the deal they'd struck with Manero Triple X. If nothing went wrong, it could be that all their troubles were solved.

When the bus stopped at the University, Luke and Tony stood. Emily would ride as far as Bailey's, where her uniform and a long evening shift awaited.

Luke's lips brushed hers. He and Tony were going to her place, where another NAIL shoot would take place. He took her briefcase.

'You look tired, baby,' she whispered.

'You too,' he said.

With that, he was gone.

Chapter Eleven

Bailey's was, as usual on a Friday night, packed.

Emily hadn't had time to prepare two outfits for Friday so her uniform wasn't as crisp and clean as it should be, but at least she had a fresh apron to cover the front of her black pants and tight white cotton shirt. Hopefully, Rhonda was managing and the owner was somewhere, anywhere, else. But it seemed all her luck for the day had been used up in Manero's office. As soon as she hit the floor she saw him, Mr Bailey Senior, no less, bending to share in the 'tasting of the wine' with a rich young starlet Emily had gone to high school with and her companion, an equally young crooner who'd just gone platinum. Their laughter mingled with the melody that rippled from the strings of a harp, plucked by the long, nimble fingers of a beautiful harpist in a black Yves Saint Laurent gown.

Real movie stars. Real artists. Real executives. For the first time in many years, she was nervous about serving the clientele. She didn't feel like the best waitress in town any more, nor did she glow with the inner knowledge that someday those stars would be sitting at her table while she held court. She felt, like her uniform, a little bit soiled.

Mr Bailey watched her like a hawk all night. In truth, her performance had been in a steady decline all summer. Attaining the Saturday night shift had been a triumph that heralded the beginning of the end. She knew it, every time a champagne cork flew across the room or a plate of appetisers slipped from her fingers to shatter on the ceramic tile. In some restaurants everyone cheered when a poor staffer dropped a plate, but not here. Movie stars and their people met here for a quiet meal. They didn't want to be looked at, bothered for autographs, or annoyed by crashing plates and an apologetic waitress, no matter how pretty that waitress might be. Yes, she knew it when it happened but she forgot it again as soon as she dragged herself out the door at the end of the night.

She could only hope a few of her regulars would pop in, greet her by name and ask to be seated at her table. *Where the hell was that Lothario Jack with his unmistakable grin and gravelly voice when she really needed him?*

Her shift was drawing to a close when a fading starlet with skin so tight it looked shrink-wrapped arrived with her entourage. Emily approached the table. She could feel the old lady's irritation with her youth as soon as she got close enough to smell the bitch's perfume.

Emily's nostrils twitched. *How could anyone make Chanel No 5 stink? Did she fucking bathe in it?*

'What do I get with the special?' The question came before Emily could open her mouth.

'With the special, you get your choice of soup or salad.'

'And what do I get with the lamb?'

'It comes with tiny new potatoes with a butter and basil roux –'

'I don't like basil,' hissed the woman, as if Emily had insulted her. 'What do I get with the sea bass?'

Emily sneezed. 'Excuse me please, miss.'

The woman's eyes widened as much as possible, given the way they'd been stretched back to her ears. 'I should think so! Now what do I get with the baked chicken?'

'Look, you get your food, you get your bill and you get out, OK?'

Not surprisingly, it was not the faded star but Emily who got out, never to be welcomed back.

* * *

Emily approached the walk-up where she lived. She hadn't really stopped laughing since the moment she'd uttered the sentence that spelled the end of her job at Bailey's. She knew she should be desolate but every time she pictured the look on the face of the old boot as she'd tried and failed to shriek (something Emily dimly recalled she'd once been quite famous for) Em had been giggling like the dumb blonde who came to Hollywood and screwed the writer to get ahead. She couldn't wait to tell Luke.

Before she started up the stairs, she was stopped by the superintendent, the usually amiable Mr Foo. His brows were knit in an angry scowl. His small frame shook with fury.

'You!'

'Why hello, Mr Foo. How are you?' Emily turned at the foot of the stairs.

'Not happy.'

'I'm so sorry.' Emily started up the stairs, her platform peep toes slowing her attempt at a speedy ascent. 'I had a long night so if you'll excuse me I'll be on my way. Goodnight.'

He followed. 'You used to be good girl,' he said.

Emily kept climbing, though her spirits sank with every word he spoke.

'No good no more. Bad girl!'

'I pay my rent on time, I never have parties –'

'Somebody have big party when you are not home.'

Em paused at her door to unlock it. She could only hope for the best as she swung it open. *Their problems were solved, provided nothing went wrong.* She should never have had that fate-provoking thought.

It looked like a shot from *Caligula*. Bodies were scattered across her couch and living-room floor, some scantily clad, and Marion (it *would* be Marion, wouldn't it!) completely naked. Beer bottles and empty pizza cartons littered the table. The camera and the clapboard with *Fuck Me Sweet and Wet* chalked on it (was it even slightly possible that Mr Foo couldn't read English?) provided ample proof of what was going on.

'See,' said Emily sweetly, 'no party!'

When she finally closed the door to Mr Foo, she held an eviction notice in her hand. Emily trod carefully, doing her best to avoid stepping on body parts, no matter how much she wanted to. She found Jillian curled up behind the sofa, cuddling a half-full beer the way a child might cuddle a stuffed toy. Emily toed her production secretary, none-too-gently.

'What?' mumbled the girl. She batted ineffectually at Emily's foot.

'Did you get it in the can?'

'What?'

'*Fuck Me Sweet and Wet*. Jillian! Did you get the fucking movie in the can?'

'Yeah ...' Jillian rolled over to face the wall, spilling the last of the beer in the process.

You can thank your lucky stars for that, bitch.

Emily approached the bedroom. She opened the door slowly, afraid of what she might find. Luke was not in the living room, which meant he was either not in the apartment at all, waiting for her in her bed or ...

There were two bodies on the bed. Em's eyes blurred

with tears. *Goddam it*. She swiped at her eyes with an impatient hand. Luke was half under the covers. With him, on top of the covers, dirty bare feet on the pillow beside Luke's head, face practically pressed against Luke's protruding feet, lay Paul.

Emily's giggles returned. For a moment she considered sliding in between the two boys-with-big-dicks but decided against it. Instead, she quickly changed into a T-shirt, jeans and sneakers, grabbed her face cream from the nightstand, and left Luke and Paul to their slumber.

The eviction noticed was posted to the inside of the front door, accompanied by a note written in black felt pen:

Anybody who leaves before this place is spotless is fired.
- Emily Forrester, Executive Producer, NAIL Productions Ltd.

Emily locked the apartment door behind her and took the back stairs out. She was experiencing a strong sense of forgiveness, of reconciliation, of love, even, for the only mother she'd ever known. *Bobby, Mommy, I'm home!*

Chapter Twelve

The Muggery rocked and The Muggery rolled. It was Saturday night and the place was packed. Luke winced at the noise, sipped his ginger ale and thanked God for the day-old pretzels. The hangover he'd woken with was passing. He could only hope that, in time, the mortification he felt at having spent the night in bed with Paul would pass as well.

Marion dragged a chair over and wedged it between him and whoever he was sitting beside. She was as peppy as ever.

'Hey, Skywalker.'

'Go away. I hate you.'

'Because I can drink like a sailor and never get a hangover?' She gulped from her mug of draught, lowered it and sighed with exaggerated contentment.

'Yes. Leave me alone.'

'No can do. Boss Lady says we're to meet her here at zero eight hundred. Or is that zero eighteen hundred? Midnight is twenty-four, right? So eight p.m. is —'

'Please …' Luke shoved the pretzels aside to make room for his elbows. He sunk his face into his palms. 'I think I might be dying.'

'Well, at least you'll die happy. You know, because you got to experience the love-that-dare-not-speak-its-name.' This last line was delivered in a teasing whisper.

'Bitch.'

'I hear his dick is a monster. Is it true? I already know yours is.'

'Don't tell me there's actually someone on campus you haven't fucked?'

'He's on my no-fly zone. Check the list.' Marion cast a snooty glance at Paul, seated as far from Luke as possible, looking even more miserable than his bedmate of the night before. 'You know, guys in Europe sleep together all the time. It's really no big deal.'

'I'm going to get better, just long enough to kill you. And then I'm going to go lie on the beach until I die.'

'Nasty.' Marion drained her mug. 'Oh barkeep!' She swung her index finger, including all the people at the Movie Mob's table. 'A round on me.' She giggled. Since there were only a handful of students at the table and less than half drinking beer, the round would be a cheap one. 'Look alive, Lucas. Here comes the E.P. her own self.'

Luke kept his face in his hands. 'How does she look?'

'She's smiling.'

'You're kidding.'

'Nope.'

Luke dared to hope. He rubbed his face and lifted it from his hands. Emily squeezed and wriggled her way straight across the dance floor. She looked ... clean. Fresh. Prettier, *far prettier*, than any star: porn, film, North. He grinned.

She grinned back.

He framed her face with his fingers, as he'd done when he'd sat in the café where she'd worked, waiting for her to love him. He couldn't sit still. Luke slid back his chair and squirmed onto the dance floor to meet her.

His arms opened and Emily stepped into his embrace. They swayed, neither dancing nor standing, just holding on tight.

'I'm sorry,' he murmured.

'Shh.' Emily put her finger to his lips. 'Bailey's fired me,' she said. She licked his neck and he felt giggles ripple from her belly, up between her breasts and out of her mouth, tickling his secret hot spot.

'Why?'

'I can't say, because if I do I won't be able to stop giggling and I don't want to giggle. I want to kiss,' she replied.

'And you're evicted.'

'Yeah. Plus I caught my boyfriend in bed with another man.'

She was giggling so hard he had to hold her tighter to keep her from doubling over.

'Emily are you – drunk? Or *on* something?'

She licked the rim of his ear. Her words were a whisper. 'I'm *in* something, Luke. I'm in love.'

Luke picked her right up off the ground and kissed her till his knees buckled.

Emily slid down his body until her feet touched the dance floor again. She pressed her belly hard against his erection.

'Let's get out of here,' Luke said. 'I've got a surprise for you at our place.'

'Not yet, baby,' she replied. She took a half-step back and waited for his erection to subside before dragging him by the hand to their table. 'I have news for NAILs!'

Luke jerked his head at Marion and she vacated her chair so Emily could sit beside her man.

'Brewski? It's on Marion,' piped up Jillian. She giggled when Marion rolled her eyes.

Emily shrugged: 'Why not?' She took the proffered mug and slugged back a healthy mouthful. 'Tastes good. Although I have to say, I'm not nuts about the stink it leaves behind – you know, when it's spilled all over everything.' She glared from face to face until each of the NAIL cast and crew members' faces burned bright red.

'As you know, I've been evicted. I stopped by the place on my way here. For a bunch of drunks, you did a good job cleaning up. Foo is considering giving me some of my damage deposit back.'

'We got the picture in the can,' piped up Jillian.

'Yeah, so you said last night.'

Jillian's face told the story – she had no memory of speaking to Emily the previous evening. 'Um ... right.'

Emily caught Paul's eye. The black man rubbed his bald pate. 'Sleep well?' she asked.

'Not too bad, actually, until I dreamed I was drowning and woke up to find a couple of hairy toes up my nose.'

'Did you wiggle your big toe?' Richard asked Luke, quoting The Bride from *Kill Bill*.

At that, the entire table, including Emily, burst into laughter.

Luke exchanged rueful glances with Paul. It was going to take a long time for them to live down the way they'd landed when the combination of exhaustion and beer had knocked them flat out on the same goddam bed. All he could do was shake his head.

Emily said, 'I got good news, good news and good news.'

She filled everyone in on the meeting between Naked And In Love Productions Limited and Manero Triple X Adult Film Distribution.

They cheered.

Tony said, 'Emily played poor Uncle Vito like a violin, man.'

'Like a Stradivarius,' said Emily. 'He's a real gentleman.'

Luke said, 'Whatever. The man did not know what hit him.'

Em grinned and nodded her head to scattered applause. 'We're launched. August first is days away. That's when the rest of the Mob should arrive.'

'I got some ideas,' said Richard. 'You know how Tarantino –'

Everybody groaned.

'No listen, I think you might like this,' he persisted. 'You know how Tarantino revitalised John Travolta's career with *Pulp Fiction*? And Pam Grier's, with *Jackie Brown*?'

Everyone nodded.

'I'd like to try doing something like that for some of the younger porn stars who came and went too fast. Track 'em down, you know, and bring them back to a new audience.'

Emily looked at Luke.

He nodded. 'Why not? There's no budget for it, though. We got squat. Especially now that Em –'

'I've left Bailey's,' said Emily, smoothly cutting him off. 'That's my second good news. I'll be working full time on NAIL until school starts. We have to make initial payments on everybody's tuition or this whole thing is a waste of time.'

Luke shook his head. 'I don't know, baby.'

'That's because I haven't told you the third part of my good news. After I left my apartment last night I went to Beverly Hills, where my stepmom lives. Or lived.'

'Lived?' Luke gave her a questioning look.

'Bobby's gone, Luke. Nothin' there but a stack of bills and a little note that said, "Gone to business meetings. Then home until Christmas." I'm assuming by "home" she means Brazil.' Emily looked around the table. 'Nobody's living at the big house in the Hills with the swimming pool and the sauna and all those empty bedrooms just waiting for –'

'Movies!' crowed Tony.

'Fuckin' right,' said Emily. She batted her lashes at Luke, probably because he'd told her he got a kick out of hearing her swear. 'Movies. Production facilities for NAIL and rooms for everyone. Now, there are a few unpaid bills that have to be covered and we'll have to keep on paying them as long as we're living there. And we've got to get our stuff moved in, somehow. But no more big rents for crappy housing, people. In no time, we'll be generating income to pay our dues and produce more movies, and so on, and on, and fuckin' on!'

Luke stared at her. It was true that he'd gotten a kick out of hearing her utter a four-letter word back when it rarely happened. But these days she was as foul-mouthed as everybody else. Now little Emily, the shy one who needed her own space, had just offered her home to six people at the table and whoever returned in August for a blitz of porn shoots before the start of school. A sharp pang almost made him gasp out loud, but he stifled it in time. *Heartache?*

Emily favoured him with a fabulous grin. Clearly, she was proud of the way she'd found a solution to all their problems. Em reached into her pocket and produced the Navajo bracelet. 'Oh Gods of Film …' she began, holding the bracelet up.

'Oh Gods of Film …' chanted the others, between snorts and giggles.

'Smile down upon us …'

Ouch. There it was again. OK, so he'd had another idea, one that was a lot simpler and involved just the two of them. He'd planned to ask her to come live with him in the house he'd called his home for three years. She could finish her Business degree, get her trust fund and finish film school the following year. Easy. Much, much easier than what was going on now. But it was obviously too late for that.

Everyone but Luke chattered excitedly. Ideas for scripts and predictions of which students would shortly return and which ones wouldn't caused the Movie Mob's table to create the kind of rumble The Muggery had been used to before the tuition hike had stifled their enthusiasm.

Eric, the owner, brought over a free pitcher of beer. 'What you kids need is a van. I've got one you can have – for a price.'

'Name it,' challenged Emily.

'I want an executive producer's credit.'

'For a van? No fuckin' way, pal,' she replied.

'You got music?' Eric nodded at the band on stage. 'A lot of new bands start out right here. I could get them for a song. Got plenty of demo CDs.'

'Original music would be good,' piped up Marion.

Emily shot her a dirty look. 'I'm the only E.P., Eric. A producer's credit is possible ... if you'll also consider investing in our prod. co.'

'You drive a hard bargain.'

Emily drained her mug and held it out for a refill.

Luke watched as Emily and Eric locked eyes. It was no surprise to him that Eric was the first to cave.

'OK, but ... maybe I might like to participate as an actor.'

'I'll let you know if we ever need an ugly middle-aged guy,' responded Emily.

Only Luke noticed the dismay that flashed across Eric's admittedly unusual face before the bar owner chuckled along with the students.

Eric patted the front of his jeans. 'I got a surprise package for you that just might change your mind.'

The Movie Mob's hilarity reached a fever pitch.

Luke sighed.

'You OK, baby?' Em touched his arm.

He smiled. 'Sure. Maybe a little heartburn.' He pushed

the stale pretzels away and sipped his ginger ale. 'It's nothing serious. I'm ready to go, though. As soon as you are.'

Her disappointment showed. 'Just a little longer? I'm having fun.'

'Come to my place when you're ready. I'll be waiting for you there.'

'OK.' Emily gave him a quick, hard kiss and turned her attention back to the Mob, most of who were peppering her with questions.

Luke launched himself into the crowd, making a beeline for the front door. Maybe all he really needed was a little fresh air.

Chapter Thirteen

Emily was feeling what Bobby called 'priddy giddy' by the time she and Marion arrived at the big old house at the edge of campus.

They each grabbed a mug of water and mounted the stairs. Emily stopped on the second-floor landing while Marion continued climbing to her room on the third.

'G'night, boss,' she said. She took her free hand from the banister in order to clumsily salute Em and spilled half her water on the floor. 'Oops. I should clean that up.' She continued climbing, her free hand once again firmly gripping the banister. 'Somebody could slip on that and take a terrible fall.'

Emily quietly opened the door to Luke's room. She'd expected to find the room dark and Luke fast asleep in his bed. But that was not the case. The room was lit for a shoot. A camera on a tripod was aimed at the bed. Luke was naked but he was lying on top of the covers and he was wide awake.

'Hi, honey, I'm home,' said Em. 'I thought you'd be fast asleep.'

'The walk revived me. I set the equipment up before I went to the bar, to surprise you. What do you think?'

Em tried to choose her words carefully but, though she was far from hammered, she was equally as far from sober.

'I don't know. It's ... gosh, it's been a while, huh?'

'Yeah! Take off your clothes, baby. I want you warm and naked and in my bed. Pronto. Spit spot, as my old nanny used to say.'

'Your nanny was Mary Poppins?' Em stripped. Before she joined him, she took the scarf hanging from the inside doorknob and tied it around the outside knob.

'A kid can dream,' he replied. 'Switch the camera on before you get in, OK?'

'Sure.' Em did as he asked and climbed into bed.

Luke cuddled her close. He smelled like mint toothpaste and guy soap and Luke.

'You're so clean!' She giggled.

'Yeah but I wanna get dirrrrrty,' he sang.

'You want to do the "Time Warp" again?'

'Oh baby, you bet. See –' he started dropping warm kisses all over her body, interspersed with words '– while I was cleaning up the disaster *your people* made of your apartment, I started wondering, How did we get into this mess in the first place?' Kisses, quick and soft as

110

whispers, landed on her cheeks, lips, eyelids and neck. 'And I remembered it all started right here. Me, recording us, making love.' Kisses crisscrossed her breasts until his lips found her nipples and his tongue joined the fun. 'But ever since NAIL began, our private movie shoots stopped. Ironic, don't you think?'

Emily nodded. She stroked his thick black hair. 'You're so gorgeous,' she said. 'You oughta be in movies.'

'Mmm.' He teased her nipples, still kissing, still licking, but sucking, too. 'Maybe,' he said, 'but I ain't gonna be.' His teeth nibbled her blushing nipples to hard nubs.

'No?' Emily arched her back as sparks of pleasure shot from each flushed tip to deep inside her belly, sending short messages, like tweets, to her clit. 'Mmm. Feels so good.' *Probably looks good, too …*

'No.' He lifted his head to look at her. His blue eyes were dark with desire. 'Except, of course, for our personal viewing.'

'Pity,' said Em. She grasped his semi-erect cock. 'Because there's a lot, right here, that would drive the ladies wild.'

'Too bad for the ladies,' he replied. He licked a line from her cleavage to her pussy. 'This is the only pussy I want,' he said. 'And I want it wet – oh, how about that? My first wish has already come true.'

He reached for the jar of Kama Sutra oil and pulled the cork with his teeth.

'Do we need it?' Emily's voice was husky. She couldn't remember the last time they'd made love, never mind the last time they'd recorded it.

'It's not for you, it's for me,' he said. He handed her the bottle. 'Lube my cock.'

Emily poured a generous amount of the exotic, spicy oil into her hand. She began to stroke him with long, slow, firm strokes, the way he liked it best.

'Sixty-nine?' she asked hopefully.

He shook his head. 'Roll over, baby,' he whispered. There was a definite edge to his quiet voice.

Emily obeyed. 'Careful?' She liked it doggy-style but in this position his cock travelled deep inside her and if it hit her cervix hard enough the strange sensation freaked her out.

Luke took his time arranging his pillows so she was well supported as she knelt up on the bed. He tucked a pillow under her face. 'Comfy?'

'Yes,' she said.

'Face the camera, Em. I don't think we caught your reply.'

There was most definitely an edge to his voice. Emily turned her face on the pillow and spoke clearly, staring straight into the lens. 'Yes, Luke, I'm comfy. I'm also really fucking close –'

'Good.'

Luke knelt behind Emily. He spread her knees wide

and began tonguing her pussy in slow, shallow strokes, starting at her clit and sliding, just between her labia, to the bottom of her opening. 'You're practically gushing,' he said. 'We may make a squirter out of you yet.'

'Uh-huh,' she said. 'Fuck, Luke, I'm so close ...'

He sat up suddenly. 'I want you to stop swearing all the time, Emily. You say "fuck" when we're fucking, OK? Not in every second sentence that comes out of your lovely mouth. Understand?'

Emily looked over her shoulder. 'Are you?'

'Yes.' Luke replied. 'You?'

'Uh-huh.'

He sat back on his heels, idly sliding one finger the length of her cunt, dipping in a little deeper when he got to her hole but not. Quite. In.

'It's just ... that's how they talk in The Business. You know?' she said.

Luke removed his hand.

Goddam him! Although ... the way he was controlling her was messing with her head and making her cunt actually ache with need.

'Please, baby ... please, um, put your big cock in my cunt and ...' *She'd been writing this stuff for months and it was still hard for her to talk dirty in bed. Fuck!*

'You haven't answered my question.'

Emily's mind went completely blank. The only clarity was in her cunt as short, hard, futile little spasms grasped

113

at nothing. *What the fuck was his question, something about squirting or – right! No swearing in public.*

'Only in bed!' she shouted, as triumphant as a game show competitor who'd been first to figure out the right answer. *Now give me my prize!*

'Good.'

Luke slipped the head of his cock into her. 'Remember how hard it was for us to fuck, at first. My big cock and your little pussy hole?'

'Uh-huh.'

'But see how easy it is, now?' He fed her hungry cunt another inch.

'Uh-huh.'

'That's how it'll be with your ass,' he said, adding, 'Mrs Bottomsby.'

She felt the warm oil dribbling between her ass cheeks. 'Lukey … oh God … not tonight.'

'You said we could try again,' he reminded her.

'Lukey … please … I'm so close.'

'I know.' He dipped to cup her clit with his palm. 'But if you come now you're not going to let me even try. I know you, Emily.'

'I'll try next time.'

'This time.' He started sliding out of her pussy again but, at the sound of her despairing moan, relented. Instead, he slid smoothly up inside her. At the same time, a finger pressed against the entrance to her ass.

114

Emily began to shake. She did not like that finger shoving its way up her ass but she loved, she *loved*, the way his cock pumped in and out and his palm pressed hard against her clit. Or maybe she did like that finger up her ass. It was moving in rhythm with his cock now, both entrances, empty only moments ago, now full.

'There's my pretty girl,' he said. 'There's my angel Emily.'

'I love you, Luke,' she whimpered.

'Ha!' A second fingertip nudged inside beside the first.

Emily threw back her head and screamed at the top of her lungs. 'It hurts!'

'Go with it, Em. You can do it.' He pushed hard with both fingers.

'No! Stop! Luke!' Emily's hands clawed the bedclothes in a futile attempt to escape.

'Christ!' Luke withdrew the second finger. He matched the rhythm of cock and finger, front and back, and fucked her furiously. 'Christ on a stick!'

Emily came as fast and wild as a mistral becomes a sudden storm.

'Ow! Ow! Fuck!' Emily's climax was never-ending, which was good because the fat dome of Luke's cock kept bumping against her cervix and it seemed as if only her paroxysms protected her womb from penetration.

She knew, probably because of the pressure of his finger up her ass, the moment his cock began to pulse as he peaked, just in time to spare her life. 'That's it, Lukey!' Emily shrieked, spurring him on, urging him to make this messy, mixed-up, fabulous fuck end before it killed her.

Luke howled. His thick cock shuddered inside Emily. His finger, buried up her bum hole, trembled.

'Oh. Dear. God,' Emily groaned.

Luke slid his limp dick from her drowned cunt. His finger slipped from her ass.

They fell apart, like two halves of a piece of exotic fruit, sliced once by a deadly blade.

The door opened. Marion stepped into the room. 'What the fuck?'

Emily started to laugh, that same laugh that had been with her since she'd been fired. She wiped the tears from her face with a corner of the tangled sheet and tried to cover herself with it.

'Too loud?' asked Luke.

'Um. Yeah.' Marion focused on Emily. 'You OK?'

Emily could see a few curls of Marion's bright red pussy hair, peeking out from under a black T-shirt with SLUT written across it in hot pink letters. She giggled. 'Uh-huh.'

'I'll have you know,' said Marion haughtily, 'I draw the line at snuff films.'

Luke and Emily clung to each other as they burst into howls of laughter.

'Say, that *is* good to know!' Luke managed to get the

words out between bursts of laughter. 'You should put that in writing so we don't forget.'

'Ha ha.'

Emily crawled to the camera. She swivelled it towards Marion and pulled focus as best she could. 'Say it again. Please, Marion!'

'Fuck you.' Marion gave the camera the finger. The hoity-toity redhead tossed her head in contempt as she turned her back to the couple. This caused her T-shirt to ride up, exposing the swell of her bum. She slammed the door behind her.

Emily switched the camera off. 'Pity,' she said. She turned off the light and cuddled up against Luke, her back to his belly. 'I'm so fu– I'm so tired.'

'Mmm.' Luke threw his arm around her waist and spooned her.

Dark. Silence. Warmth.

Post-orgasmic bliss.

Emily sank into sleep like a skipping stone, after the final skip, sinks into the sea.

Chapter Fourteen

Luke sat in a patio chair, beyond splashing distance from the pool. The Film Department had given him absolute orders to relinquish the University's equipment immediately or risk being fined.

Emily sat across from him, yakking on the phone and making notes.

A few members of the Movie Mob, following Emily's instruction to drive the neighbours, who'd started frequenting their back yards again since Bobby's departure, indoors once more, frolicked naked in the pool. *Pool Party* would be shot as soon as they could be fairly sure there'd be no nosy neighbours spying on their activities. The rest of the newest inhabitants of Beverly Hills ate, slept, steamed or made out in the various rooms of the big house.

Most of the missing Mob members had returned on 1st August to continue working with NAIL and had been more than happy to move into Bobby's house. Blaine was a no-show but he'd already provided what they'd needed most from him – the shell company Emily had turned into their prod. co.

Jimmy, Director of Photography, also didn't return, but Paul filled the position nicely. Unfortunately, Patricia, who'd been screwing Professor Simmons, was also a no-show. Which was why Luke's possession of the University's cameras was no longer being overlooked by the head of the department.

Luke admired his gorgeous girl. She looked every inch the star in her, well, *Bobby's*, Ferragamo sunglasses and Stella McCartney one-piece bandeau bathing suit. He grinned. *The things you learn shooting porn* ... Last year he hadn't known Paul McCartney's daughter was a famous designer. Now he liked to think he could pick out one of her creations by the way it draped the body and the ease with which it could be removed.

Things were going swimmingly. He chuckled out loud. Emily had kicked up a bit of a fuss at his insistence on keeping his room at the house, but he'd held his ground. He wasn't ready to pull up roots and it wasn't as if he could change his mind once he left. There was a waiting list for rooms in that house that was longer than a half-hour porn script. Not that a half-hour porn script, even a half-hour NAIL porn script, was all that long.

Part of Emily's objection, he suspected, was Marion's refusal to give up her third-floor attic room.

Emily was jealous, pure and simple. As far as he knew she knew nothing of his one-time arrangement with Marion, which had been fun while it lasted and had ended the day he'd laid eyes on Em. He was darn sure Marion hadn't talked. She had a big mouth, all right, but not when it came to talking, just sucking. He shook his head to clear his mind before his cock got any harder. Friends with benefits, fuck-buddies, whatever he and Marion had been, they were pals now. Colleagues and pals.

He glanced around idly. The redhead wasn't hard to spot. She was roaming what Em called 'the back forty', tracking songbirds with her recording equipment. He and Em had argued about that, too, but Em had won out. For now, much as Marion loved sound, she was First Assistant Director. Emily thought Marion's looks and personality were poorly suited to recording and editing sound. Luke could see her point but … just watching the joy on Marion's face as she captured the trilling of a little chickadee, or whatever it was, made it clear, at least to him, that if she got what she wanted she'd end up in sound.

It *was* time to put her in front of the camera, though. That much he and Emily agreed on. But Emily hadn't written anything yet and neither had Marion so …

He tucked the lenses in their protective pouches and placed them gently in the camera case. He had absolutely no idea where they'd get cameras from until school started up again. But that wasn't his problem.

He stood. Time to get these cameras back to campus. He gave Emily a wave but she shook her head, motioning him back into his seat. Obediently, he sat. It looked like she was almost ready for another 'Me Tarzan, you Jane' lesson but he was hesitant to go there. Besides, everything that wasn't directly related to NAIL slipped from her mind in days. It wasn't as if he wanted to dominate her, necessarily. He just didn't want her pussy-whipping him. There was a big difference between the two.

Emily hung up. She told Luke, 'Good news! Vito says it's all selling like hotcakes. The *Young Love* trilogy, with Tony and Aileen, has gone viral. All the porn sites that are owned by women, and it seems that there are a lot of them, want it because it's romantic as well as very sexy. That's a whole new market. They want NAILs' inventory on their sites ASAP. Hah!' She pumped the air in triumph.

'Fantastic!' Luke said. 'Did he have any suggestions for more?'

'Plenty! Interracial. Your bed-buddy, Paul? It's time to take him out from behind the camera and put him in front of it. Vito wants some three-girl action, but again, as romantic as we can make it.'

'Romantic? Three-way love as well as lust?'

'Why not? For it to work, we need three girls who are not only willing to do lesbian stuff, but who are into each other. That might be tricky.'

'Anything else?'

'Some older woman/younger guy. Cougars are in fashion, in porno, it seems. Young guys, we got lots of. Any ideas for older women?'

Luke mused. 'I can think of some lady profs who are crazy enough to consider it and some who'd look great on camera. Unfortunately, none that has both the looks and the willingness.'

Emily shrugged. 'The man wants cougars, cougars he shall have. Find me one, Luke.'

'I have to get these cameras back to campus.'

'What are we going to use if you turn in our equipment?'

'I told you about this, Emily. I turn in the equipment or they start fining me.'

'Fuck.' She turned her attention to her calculator and started bashing away at it.

Mind like a sieve ... Luke glowered. The girl remembered nothing he taught her but every word Vito Manero uttered was memorised, analysed and jotted down in her journal.

'We'll have to rent some.' She looked up. 'Would it be cheaper to just pay the fines and hang on to the cameras we have?'

'Probably. But it makes me look bad, Em.'

'I can't imagine anything could make you look bad, gorgeous,' she said.

Was she playing him?

'Lukey, don't turn in the cameras today. Go get a cougar, please?'

'Just like that? Where? How?'

'I don't care where or how or what it takes, just do it.'

'No matter what?'

'No matter what.'

Luke said, 'But, Emily …'

'Just do it, OK?'

'You're the boss.' *For now, little girl.*

'Yes, I am. He also wants some very big dicks so keep your eyes open.'

'So when I'm not prowling cougar bars you want me to hang out in men's rooms looking for cock?'

'Not cock. Big cock!' She grinned.

'You're losing your mind,' said Luke. He slung the camera case over his shoulder.

'Just like a real producer!' she crowed. 'All I'm asking is that you keep your eyes open. So far we've only got Paul and supposedly Eric. But Eric's tests aren't back yet so he's out. And you, of course but …'

'But I'm the director.'

'Right. So forget about the big cock thing if you want, just please, Mr Director, go do some cougar casting. Ask Tony. He knows all kinds of stuff. Just make sure she's pretty, hmm? It'd be super if her health records are up to date, too. Otherwise we'll have to use condoms which is OK but not ...' Her voice trailed off as she turned her attention back to her laptop.

Luke waited for her to finish her sentence.

She started tapping at her keyboard.

Luke growled. 'Will that be all, Mr Weinstein?'

Emily looked up, obviously surprised he was still there. A beach ball bounced across the courtyard. She whacked it away from the patio table. 'Working over here!' she yelled. 'See you later?' she asked.

'I think I'll go home tonight. Turn in the camera equipment in the morning.' He started to walk away.

'Luke?'

He stopped. 'Yes?'

She gave him a pretty little baby pout.

That's more like it. He waited for her to beg him to come back to the house later, so they could fall asleep in each other's arms.

'Please don't turn in the cameras yet. Pretty pretty please?' She batted her lashes.

Luke was so surprised he actually laughed – the sound as short and harsh as a big dog's bark. 'OK. You know where to find me when you want me,' he said.

Emily flexed her fingers. 'I'm going to write such a scorching hot script for your cougar and Paul you'll need the Ove Glove just to hold it in your hand. We'll get big dick plus interracial plus cougar. Vito will be in heaven!' She turned her attention back to her laptop. 'Bye, Luke.'

'Yep,' he said.

'Remember, whatever it takes.' Em started tapping at her keyboard again. 'Marion,' she called, oblivious to the redhead only yards away from her, 'where are you?' When she received no answer she upped her volume. 'Marion! I need you! NOW!'

***

Luke found Tony in the sauna.

'There's a place downtown – Cheetahs – where the cougars hang out,' said Tony. He was lying on a towel with another towel draped across his torso.

Oh well, I already know the size of his cock. Luke closed his eyes. He mopped his brow. *Things are getting out of hand …*

'There is?' he said. 'Great! What do we do, put a notice up in their ladies' room?'

Tony shook his head. 'Emily said whatever it takes, right?'

'Right.' Luke swiped at his face again.

'What it'll take is one of us going there and propositioning some of these older ladies.' Tony stretched his arm so he could grab a ladle and pour cold water over hot, fake rocks. He rolled over onto his belly. As the room filled with even more steam, he made a pillow of the towel that had covered his privates and tucked it under his head. His ass was bare. 'Ahh. This is heaven.'

Gross.

'You?' Luke was seized with a sense of desperation. He *had* to get out of the sauna and away from this house.

'Not me. You. You and Richard.' Tony's voice was muffled by his makeshift pillow.

'The Tarantino freak? Why him?'

'He's big on older women. You should see his collection of what he calls "the golden age of porn" tapes. Richard says they were all in it for the fun of it, not the money. He says you can see it in their eyes.' Tony's voice slowed. His eyelids drooped. 'Maybe he can pick out the right kind of cougar for us.'

'I'll ask him, then.' Luke, practically gasping for air, swung the door to the sauna open. 'Print us up another batch of business cards, OK?'

'Now?' Tony's eyes opened.

'Yeah now,' snapped Luke. 'Christ, man, wake up already! It's the middle of the fucking day!'

Tony stood, wrapping a towel around his dripping body. 'Yes, sir!'

Chapter Fifteen

That night, after carefully preparing for their assignment at their house, Luke and Richard showed up at Cheetahs. It was just after ten p.m. Despite their business cards, fresh-faced and crew-cut Richard had to show ID. The bouncer grinned. 'These she-cats'll eat you up, sonny, looking like that.' The chubby-cheeked boy was dressed preppy: loafers, chinos, pale-pink shirt and an Argyle pullover sweater with pink in the pattern, contrasting with Luke's Doc Marten's, black jeans and tight black T-shirt. Between them, they figured, they had the market covered.

They bought two beers for ten dollars each. The barkeep told them, 'Don't worry. Most of your drinks will be bought for you, if you play your cards right.'

They found a booth and scanned the room. The patrons weren't all older women and younger men.

Luke nodded towards a table with two people, a couple who were likely in their mid-forties, maybe married. 'What do think they're doing here, Rich?'

'Looking for a young stud for her, with him watching them do it, or else for a threesome.'

'I don't know how I'd feel about going home with a man and a woman. It seems kinda creepy to me.'

'Different strokes, Luke. Still, I agree. If they were all friends, before, I think that'd be OK, but being picked up by a couple of complete strangers sounds kinda risky, to me, 'specially if it's a big guy.'

Among the throng, there were a few older men and younger women, but the clientele was predominantly women in their forties and men in their twenties.

'Makes sense,' Luke said. 'Both sexes at the ages when they're in their sexual primes.'

'Now you're getting it,' Richard said. 'Just remember, if you get one in the sack, let her teach you. Act dumb.'

'Be my pleasure.'

'This is OK with Emily?'

'She said do whatever it takes to get a cougar. If this is what it takes, it's not my fault, is it?'

'I'm on your side, bro.' Richard tapped the table with his empty bottle. 'No kind ladies are lining up to buy us drinks, Luke. Will the expense account run to another round?'

'This is my pocket, Richard, but I guess we can't sit here dry.'

At the bar, Luke ordered two more. When he picked the beaded bottles up, a husky contralto said, 'That's on my tab, Bert.'

Luke turned. His benefactress looked a well-preserved forty, with wide-spaced ice-blue eyes under long lashes and tinted eyelids. Her lips were a little thin and painted bright red. His eyes moved down. Her gold lamé top plunged to the belt buckle of black velvet Capris with gold trim. Her gilt sandals had four-inch heels.

She took a sip from what Luke assumed was an Appletini, by its colour. 'Have you

seen enough, young man?' she asked.

Luke cleared his throat. 'Not yet.'

'Bad boy?' she asked.

'Working on it.'

'Need help?'

'I wouldn't say no.'

'To what?'

'Just about anything.'

The blonde laughed, a full-blown, head-back laugh. 'I like you already, "Bad Boy". Have you a name?'

'Luke.'

She extended a hand. 'Gloria.'

'Glorious Gloria from across the pond.'

'Guilty!' Gloria laughed again. 'Fancy a bit of Brit, mate?'

Luke nodded. For the life of him he couldn't come up with a witty response.

Gloria looked at the pair of bottles in his fist. 'Hard drinker?'

'No. One's for my friend.'

She frowned. 'You're with someone? Boy or girl?'

'Boy. Richard.'

'You going to introduce me, then?'

Luke led her to the booth where Richard was waiting and made introductions. 'Well?' he asked his friend.

'I'd say so.'

Gloria said, 'It's not nice to have secret conversations. What was that all about?'

Luke answered, 'Richard thinks he can tell how ... er ... fiery a woman is by her eyes.'

She turned a smouldering look on Richard. 'And?'

'Scorching. Love your accent, too.'

Gloria grinned. 'So, what's happening, boys? You two gay and looking to experiment or what?'

They both assured her, and assured her, and assured her, that they weren't in the least bit gay.

'So what's the deal? One to hold the other's hand? We don't have a virgin here somewhere, do we?' She posed the question with relish.

'No, no virgins, sorry. Is that your thing?'

'My "thing" is my business, for now. So tell me all about yourselves.'

Luke produced his NAIL business card.

After a glance, Gloria dropped it on the table. 'Save that to impress little girls, Luke. This town is full of movie producers and directors who've never made movies.'

'I'm serious,' he assured her. 'We've only made a couple of shorts, so far, but this is how we're putting ourselves through movie school.'

Gloria picked his card up and took a closer look. '"Naked And In Love"? You kids are making porn movies?'

'Artistic ones,' Richard said.

'Hm.' She looked thoughtful.

Richard opened his mouth but Luke nudged him into silence.

'You have a full crew, cameramen, lights, sound, the whole shebang?'

'Everything,' Luke told her. 'As I said, we've already made a few movies, and sold them.'

'So they're being seen by people?'

'One trilogy has gone viral on line.'

'I'm impressed. You know, when you get a little older you start wondering if there's anything new to explore. I think while I've still got the body for it, I might enjoy a good shag captured on film.'

'It's all digital now –' began Richard but Luke cut him off.

'Our buyer has asked us for something with a younger man and a … mature … woman,' he said.

'Mature like me?'

'Exactly,' Luke told her. 'A true cougar.'

She mused. 'Kinky, at your age. What is the world coming to?'

'Well, would you?' Luke asked.

'Depends. This cougar is pedigree. Understand?'

Luke frowned. 'You mean …'

'I mean I come with papers. Health papers. Do you?'

'Absolutely,' Luke assured her. 'So, are you in?'

'Don't I have to audition first? Don't you want to see what you get?'

'Audition?'

She opened her purse and took out a key card. 'Midnight, the Tiara on Park Lane, suite one nine one one.'

Richard squeaked, 'Both of us?'

Her look passed from Luke to Richard like a flame-thrower. 'I have a big appetite.'

'We'll do our best to satisfy it,' Luke assured her.

'I'm counting on it.' She sashayed away, leaving the boys looking at each other.

An hour later, Luke paused to admire the famous back-lit four-storey cascade in the lobby of the Tiara.

Richard touched his elbow. 'It's seven minutes to twelve. We should keep moving.'

Luke shook his head. 'I don't know about this, Richard.'

'Emily?'

'Yeah.'

'She told you, whatever it takes.'

'Even so.'

'How about we play by President's rules?'

'Which are?'

'BJs don't count as sex. If Mr Penis doesn't meet Miss Vagina, in an intimate sort of way, no one has two-timed anyone. That's President Clinton's rule, which almost makes it a law.'

'And anything else goes?'

'You already shook her hand.'

'No I didn't.'

'Well, if you had, would that be sex? Would that be cheating on Emily?'

'No.'

'A peck on the cheek?'

'No.'

'If you touched her –'

Luke interrupted with, 'I get the point. You have to draw the line somewhere and we are deciding to draw it at actual penetration.'

'We're not deciding. Clinton decided. We're just following his lead,' Richard reminded him. 'And the line is drawn at *vaginal* penetration.'

'What's the –'

But Richard was already heading for the elevators, leaving Luke to think about why the word 'penetration' needed modifying.

It took three swipes of the card for Richard to get the door to 1911 open, but he wasn't used to key cards and his hand wasn't that steady. The suite was spacious, with no bed visible, so it had to have more than one room. There was a four-seater green leather couch against the wall opposite the entrance. Gloria was displayed on it.

She'd changed. Her narrow feet were tucked into pom-pom kitten-heeled red satin mules. She wore black nylons that were as sheer as shadows. The hose were held up by the suspenders of a frilly garter belt that nipped her narrow waist. Her breasts were nestled in a quarter-cup crimson satin bra. Over all, she wore a flame-tinted peignoir so fine that it did little more than glisten over her flesh. She had another Appletini in her hand.

Richard gasped. 'I think I've died and gone to heaven! *That*, Luke, is what a porn star is supposed to look like.'

'You're too kind,' Gloria purred. She turned her gaze to Luke and lifted an elegant eyebrow.

Responding to the unsubtle cue, he said, 'You look fantastic, Gloria. I really mean that.'

'How sweet. It's so nice to meet young men who've been taught good manners. A rare pleasure these days.' She topped up her glass from a vacuum pitcher.

Luke suppressed a laugh. The situation – the topic of conversation – combined with Gloria's classy English accent, was so odd it was funny and yet it was extra-sexy at the same time. He couldn't help but wonder what she'd sound like if she were vocal when she climaxed. Would she say something like, 'Jolly good show. I'd rather like another of those, if you don't mind?'

Luke thought that it'd be more polite to make some friendly conversation before ... before the three of them got started. 'You sure like those Appletinis, huh?'

'A girl needs her vitamins. "An apple a day", right? Then there's celery and tomato in a Bloody Mary, the olives in Martinis, lemon slices, orange peel twists – I believe in a healthy diet.'

The boys chuckled to show they weren't taking her seriously.

Gloria patted the couch beside her. 'One of you join me, please. The other, if you don't mind, can take the first shower.'

Richard asked, 'Shower?'

'Humour me. I do like a man's body fresh from a good hot shower. If you two don't want to be separated, you can shower together, if you like, but I'd insist on watching.'

'No, no, that's fine,' Luke assured her. 'I'll go first.' Perhaps it'd be easier getting into the threesome if Richard already had it started.

Richard made for the couch, shedding his sweater as he went. Luke headed for the bathroom. It had everything, including disposable razors and two toothbrushes still in their plastic bubbles. Luke let the water pound his skin, growing an erection when he thought about Gloria's body and what he was going to do to it, he hoped, and losing his stiffness when he remembered that he and she wouldn't be alone. He could cope with that, he thought, provided – what was the expression he'd heard? – he and Richard didn't 'cross swords'.

What if Richard's was bigger than his? Nah. Not at all likely. But ...

Ablutions finished, Luke dried off and looked for a robe. There wasn't one. He could put his worn clothes back on but that likely wasn't what Gloria wanted. In the end, he settled for knotting a big towel around his waist. It wasn't the most modest or secure garment, but what the hey!

When Luke got back to them, Richard was bare-chested but his zipper hadn't been pulled down. He was kissing Gloria and fondling one of those cute English tits of hers, though the miniscule bra was still in place. They must have been taking it slow, waiting for him.

Gloria said, 'Richard, shower. You, Luke, come here. Let's see what you have to offer a lady, shall we?'

Richard almost ran to the bathroom, his confined erection pointing the way.

Luke held on to the knot in his towel and went to where Gloria sat. Holding it did him no good. She grabbed the towel and whipped it away. To Luke's shame, he didn't have an erection, just a semi-stiff dangler.

'I ... I ...' he began.

'You're shy,' Gloria said. 'Don't worry. Gloria knows how to bring shy boys out of their shells.' She leaned forwards, cupped his balls in her palm, and breathed on the dome of his cock. 'Come on out to play with Gloria,' she told it.

Either the warmth of her breath or the proximity of his cock to her mouth had the desired effect. The top of her head was blocking his view, but he felt the swelling and stiffening and lifting and then the gentle contact as hard and glossy dome met soft and yielding lips.

'That's a miracle I never tire of watching,' Gloria said. 'From soft and limp to hard and straight, it's like some kind of magic.' She looked up at him. 'Thank you for sharing it with me, Luke.'

'You're welcome.' It was ridiculous, but somehow Luke felt touched by her words. There had been times, looking at Emily's body, when he'd felt an overwhelming tenderness for it that was even stronger than his lust. Gloria's words seemed to be trying to convey the same sort of emotion. He wanted to respond but, silly as it might be, he was too choked up to trust himself to speak.

Then Gloria kissed his cock and all emotions but lust vanished. The muscles in his bottom tensed. She pulled back. 'Let's not rush, shall we?'

'Lots of time,' he croaked.

She pulled him down beside her and tugged at the

back of his neck, drawing his lips to hers. Her tongue seemed to be memorising every contour of his mouth.

He was being kissed by a woman in her forties, a mature, very experienced woman. Every kiss he'd ever experienced before, with Emily or any other girl, had been with him in the alpha role. Even as he'd enjoyed the act of kissing, he'd always held the thought that his kisses would get the girl hot enough for him to be allowed to fondle her breasts and that, in turn, would excite her so that she'd part her thighs, and so on. These kisses were nothing like that. There was a tacit agreement between Gloria and him that he'd be free to do pretty much anything he liked with her. For once, he wasn't cast in the role of seducer. That was a liberating but peculiar feeling. And he wasn't in control of the kisses. She was. Gloria had taken over his alpha position. That took the pressure off but also diminished his male power.

Odd! Luke shrugged, mentally. He wasn't going to screw her, but one way or another he was sure he was going to get off with her. That's what really counted. *Stop thinking and start fondling, moron …*

He cupped one cool trembling breast and brushed the ball of his thumb across its tip. Gloria gave a gratifying little quiver. Caress and reaction. Luke considered it the most satisfying form of communication that humans can share.

She whispered into his ear, 'Harder, please, Luke. I like it to hurt just a little, if you don't mind.'

He pinched.

Gloria said, 'Thank you. That's nice.'

She leaned over his naked chest and nibbled at his nipple. For Luke, that wasn't an erogenous zone but he appreciated the attention nonetheless. Her palm lifted his balls. That was more like it. A pointed nail scratched just beneath his scrotum.

She was going to take him into her mouth. He was sure she was. He'd wait, though. He wouldn't ask and he wouldn't push down on the back of her head, not even very gently. Let her take her time, no matter how excruciating the anticipation was.

She asked, although it wasn't a question, 'You want me to suck your dick, don't you.'

Luke managed to grunt.

'You have to ask.'

Bitch! 'Yes, I'd like you to.'

'I will, but me first, OK?'

Luke slid off the couch to squat on the floor. His hands eased Gloria's knees apart.

'The bedroom would be more comfortable,' she said.

'OK.' He stood up, *very* aware that his cock was wagging a foot before her face. It most likely looked funny from her point of view but he was still proud of it.

'Aren't you a handsome fellow,' Gloria told his cock.

As she stood, she wrapped a fist around his shaft. Luke was led to the bedroom like that.

'How about Richard?' he asked.

'He'll find us,' she assured him.

Her peignoir slid to the floor with a slithering sound that he found incredibly erotic. She rubbed her thighs together; her stockings rasped. That was even sexier. That was the difference with older women, he guessed. Emily would never think to deliberately create those sorts of sounds. A pang of guilt clenched his belly. It was bad enough he was having sex with another woman. Disloyal thoughts just made it worse.

Gloria threw herself backwards onto a king-sized bed. She landed with her knees far apart and dangling over the edge. Her long fingers pulled the lips of her pussy apart, exposing the succulent wet flesh between them.

'A pink orchid,' Luke said. It was a compliment he'd used before but she didn't know that.

'More of a ripe and luscious fruit,' she corrected him. 'You should try it.'

Luke took the hint. He dropped to his knees and brought his face close to the glistening wetness of her core. 'Ahh!' He sucked aromatic air through his open mouth with exaggerated relish. Some girls can be nervous about odour. It's a good idea to reassure them. It helps them relax.

Yeah, like Gloria needed sexual reassurance! She'd likely been licked by a hundred older, more experienced men. They were his competition.

Her clit was much bigger than Em's. Was it because she was older? Did clits continue to grow as ... No! That was ridiculous. Cocks didn't, after all.

Gloria said, 'Thanks for the appreciation, or is it contemplation, but how about some tongue action, Luke?'

There was no putting it off. Luke surrendered to his own eagerness and buried his face into the soft, convoluted pinkness. His tongue stretched down to tickle her perineum for a few strokes before moving up to flick the edge of the little cup that was formed by the joining of her pussy's lips. It was very wet. He couldn't help but think, Her 'cup runneth over', but at least he had the sense not to say it out loud.

Gloria's body shifted, but not impatiently. She moaned softly and pushed herself up at him. Good. Luke twisted and turned his tongue, exploring inside her, left and right. The intricacy of women, inside, was totally awesome. When he fucked, he sometimes liked to imagine that the size of his cock smoothed all those folds out until the woman was smooth in there, though he knew that wasn't possible. Or was it?

Gloria gasped, 'My clit? Please?'

Now *that* is music to a man's ears. Taking advantage of the size of her clit, Luke gripped it between his lips. He nodded, shook his head and rotated it.

He was rewarded with an, 'Uh, uh, uh,' and the straining of her thighs further apart.

Luke worked a hand up between them so that he could get two fingers inside her, behind her pubic bone, to rotate on her G-spot. With her clit held firmly in his lips, he set the tip of his tongue to work on its tiny arrowhead.

Gloria said, 'There you are, Richard. What took you so long?'

Luke licked and fingered harder.

Richard said, 'I wanted to be clean for you everywhere, Gloria, so I was very thorough.'

In a conversational voice, despite what Luke was doing to her, Gloria said, 'Bring that lovely dick up where I can reach it, Richard. Or should I say, Dick, bring that Richard up here?'

She still had enough self-control to make bad jokes? Fucking Brits! He redoubled his efforts, eyes closed so he could concentrate, not because he wanted to avoid the sight of Gloria's lips wrapped around Richard's cock.

She made slurping sounds, though, and Richard started to grunt. Closing his eyes didn't stop Luke from imagining.

But Gloria was making little humping motions at his face, fucking his mouth with her clit. He sucked, hard. Maybe he could suck an orgasm right out of her.

She didn't squirt, which he'd thought she might, for some reason. Even so, one second her pussy was just very wet, the next it was *saturated*. Woman-juice dripped down his chin.

Mission accomplished!

Her gentle hands moved his head to one side. 'That was lovely, Luke. Your girlfriends must be very happy. I can't remember ever being eaten with such skill.'

Luke's face warmed at the praise. Hopefully he wasn't blushing.

Gloria cupped her mound with both hands. 'Don't worry, boys. I can come over and over, given the right lovers, and that's what I've got right now. Richard, would you mind if I fucked you? I need the exercise and fucking a boy is a far better way to work out than walking on a treadmill, don't you think?'

Richard scrambled across the bed to throw himself down beside Gloria and in much the same position. Luke backed away before standing. Gloria sat up, rolled over and threw a thigh over Richard. Her hand steered his shaft as she lowered herself. She didn't pause as he entered her. She had to be very slippery inside, thanks to Luke's superior oral skills.

Her hips rotated. 'Luke, you know what I like when I fuck?'

'No, Gloria, what do you like when you fuck?' Luke could be just as cool as she could.

'A nice big dick in my mouth. I see that you have one. Would you oblige?'

Would he? With him standing up, his cock was higher than her head. If he knelt, it'd be too low. Squatting a bit wasn't the most comfortable position, but once he did, and her lips parted for him, and the head of his cock was inside her mouth, resting on her tongue, being sucked gently and rhythmically, Luke knew that he could hold that position for an hour, or more.

The English girl worked her hips and her mouth. Luke rested a hand on top of her head but, as his lust grew, he made a fist in her hair. His other hand stroked her face. Sometimes, his fingertips could feel his cock through her cheek. She did things with her tongue that swiftly brought him to a point that ...

And then she paused. Luke resisted the urge to simply fuck her face. If she wanted to drag it out, he could live with it. This was the only time he wished he followed sports more closely. He needed base-ball statistics or something similar to keep him from exploding. Emily. *What would Em do if she walked in right now?* That did the trick. He actually felt himself soften for a moment, before Gloria brought him back to full stiffness.

She released his cock. *Fuck!* He should have come while he had the chance. Now what?

She said, 'There's a vacancy at the rear, Luke, if you'd like to fill it.'

'I can come more than once, too,' he said.

'Boys,' she said. 'Such a treat, really.' Gloria wrapped her lips around his dome again and rapidly whirled her tongue around it. She sucked his cock deeper into her mouth, still circling it with her tongue and began to nod, as if giving him permission to come.

That did it. With a grunt, Luke emptied his load in three hard, fast spurts. He fell back on the bed, sliding free of her mouth. 'Wow,' he said, panting, 'you are one talented cocksucker, lady.'

She licked her glistening lips. 'My back passage, please.'

It took him a moment to figure that out. Right. She wanted him to fuck her bum.

Richard, humping up as Gloria rode him hard, said, 'President's rules, remember, Luke.'

So that's why he'd been so specific about only vaginal sex counting as cheating. Richard had been thinking way further ahead than he had. *Fucking smartass.*

Luke got off the bed and dawdled his way around it, thinking furiously.

Gloria said, 'There's lubricant in the top drawer of the nightstand, Luke.'

He opened it. The plastic bottle, when full, must have held about a pint. It was three-quarters empty. That told a story, didn't it?

Beside the lube lay a vibrator. It was thicker and longer that his cock, with a bulbous head and a transparent body that was filled with multi-coloured beads. The vibrations it gave out had to be quite complex.

Gloria wanted to be, what did the English call it? Buggered. Fine. Luke lubed the vibrator lavishly. Gloria still gyrated on Richard's cock. Richard was pounding upwards ferociously. Luke put a palm on Gloria's lower back, to still her for a second, then applied the vibrator to her tiny pursed hole. He pushed, not hard, but inexorably. A thumb turned the gadget on. It came alive in his hand, and Gloria's bum.

Gloria squealed.

Richard let loose a torrent of, 'Fuck, fuck, fuck, fuck …'

Of course. Richard would be getting the full benefit of the vibrations through the thin membrane that separated her back entrance from her front. Luke envied him that extreme pleasure, but not enough to overcome his reluctance to cheat on Emily.

Within seconds, both Richard and Gloria climaxed, noisily. Gloria dismounted. 'Drinkies, anyone?'

Both men nodded. Gloria got up and stroked Luke's cheek. 'President's rules?' she purred.

'What?'

'Clinton, wasn't it? We do get American news on the other side of the pond, Luke, especially when it's juicy.'

Chapter Sixteen

'I just don't get it,' said Emily.

Gary and Kara had arrived and Jillian had single-handedly put together a celebratory meal of spaghetti with meatballs, Caesar salad and garlic bread. It wasn't fancy but it wasn't take-out, either, and the Movie Mob had enthusiastically tucked right in. Red wine had been consumed and, though the dishwasher was now humming quietly in the corner, the wine glasses remained full.

After a four-day drive, even the closest of lovers needed a break from each other. Gary, Tony and Paul were in the rec room, playing pool, while the girls, Kara, Jillian, Emily and Marion, lingered at the dining-room table.

'What?' Marion topped up everyone's glass and, with an expression of regret, set aside the now empty wine bottle.

'This whole preoccupation with anal sex,' replied Emily. She'd spent the day at the patio table, writing until it was too dark to see. It'd been a relief when Gary's car pulled up and she'd come inside to find a decent meal prepared and friends to dine with. If she'd had a glass or two too many of the Cabernet, well, who was counting? Besides, it was her wine, at least, it was from the wine cellar in her house, so she was entitled to drink as much of it as she liked. And she did like.

The other girls laughed but, likely noticing the serious way in which Emily looked from one to the next and the next, leaped on the topic with the kind of sincere gusto that girls-with-wine are apt to do.

Jillian went first. 'I've done it. I can't say I'm crazy about it, but my ex-boyfriend was desperate to give it a try. So I did.'

'Didn't it hurt?' Emily peered over the rim of her wine glass at the little brunette.

'Yes. We did it three times and it hurt three times. So I said I'd had enough. By then we were sort of falling apart, though. If we'd stayed together I might've tried again, but I don't miss it.' Jillian shrugged. 'Don't miss him, either.'

All four laughed together.

'It just seems so painful. And degrading. Why would anyone want to do it?' asked Em.

'Because it's painful and degrading,' said Kara. 'My favourite!' She blew out a candle that was about to start dripping on the tablecloth. 'Gary and I are into that sort of stuff. He spanks me, too.'

'If you're bad?' asked Jillian.

'Sometimes if I'm very bad. And sometimes if I'm very, very good,' said Kara.

Emily shook her head. 'I don't get it, but it'd make a great little porn movie. What do you say?'

'You'll have to ask Gary. He's the boss, with a capital B.'

'I wouldn't have guessed you guys were D/s,' said Marion. 'Dominant/submissive,' she added, when Emily and Jillian gave her uncomprehending looks.

Kara shrugged. 'Only in bed. We're not into the "lifestyle", if you know what I mean. I couldn't do it twenty-four-seven. But sometimes it's fun to be ordered around. You know, I'm always thinking, thinking, thinking. What's next for me? For us? Will I stay in LA? Will Gary and I stay together? Get married? Do I want kids? Blah blah blah. I tell you, a good caning drives all that stuff right out of your mind. You're free to just do what you're told, without thinking, or deciding, or even reciprocating. You just be. He does everything. You're just the … the object, the precious object, of his attention. It's good.'

'I don't find anal sex painful at all, any more,' said Marion. 'But caning? That's gotta hurt!'

'Like a bitch, dude,' said Kara. 'For a few strokes. Then it changes, something just changes, you know?'

The other three girls shook their heads.

'I guess it's the endorphins kicking in,' said Kara, 'and it doesn't hurt at all any more. You want it. You ride it, the way you ride a wave on your board. Then –'

'Then?' prompted Marion.

'Then either you come like a fucking house on fire or it starts to hurt like a bitch again. If that happens, if it starts to hurt, I just call out my safe word and he stops.'

'Hmm.' Marion sat back in her chair. She lit a cigarette from the pack the four girls were sharing. 'I might get off on that.'

'My mind could sure use clearing,' said Emily. 'I've got half a dozen scripts half finished. Vito's doing a great job of distribution but we need to shoot them all before September if we want to pay off the fee hike for everyone's first semester.'

'Heavy is the head that wears the crown,' said Jillian sympathetically. She rose from her spot at the table and circled round behind Emily's chair. Jillian started massaging Emily's bare shoulders. 'You're as tight as a ... a ...'

'Virgin asshole?' prompted Marion.

Emily grinned ruefully. 'I think that's the way mine is going to stay. But Luke ...'

'Mmmhmm,' muttered Marion.

'I know you and Luke were lovers before I came along,' said Emily. Her grey eyes focused sharply on Marion's face.

Marion's green eyes widened. Her face turned as scarlet as her hair. 'You do not. We weren't ... did he say ... where'd you hear that?'

Emily snorted in a very unladylike manner. 'I deduced it, Doctor Watson.'

'Is that so?' Marion frowned. 'How did you come to this conclusion, Sherlock?'

'Elementally – elementary, my friend. When I asked you to try to seduce him, to see if he really loved me, you said you "even kissed the side of his neck". Only a lover would know about his secret weakness for that.'

'Oh.'

Everyone was silent for a moment. Emily could feel all eyes on her. She laughed. 'I don't care. He wasn't my first, either.'

'We weren't lovers,' said Marion. 'We were friends with benefits. Seriously.'

Jillian kneaded harder. Emily's neck emitted an audible pop.

'Fuck, girl, you are uptight,' said Kara. She shot Marion a warning glance.

'Don't worry, I'm not going to freak out,' said Emily. 'Just be honest, please. What the fuck is the difference between friends with benefits and lovers? I want to know.'

Marion sighed. 'OK, but remember, you asked. I'm a size queen. I like a big dick. The bigger, the better. I like sucking a big one, I like fucking a big one and I like a great big dick up my ass.'

'They say only about ten per cent of women like anal sex but the ones that like it *really* like it,' offered Kara.

'Go on,' Emily prodded Marion.

'So, Luke, you know, he has a big one. And whether you do or don't agree with it, he likes anal sex. We're friends. We're housemates. When we met, we were both single. But we never went on a date or sat out on the porch talking about the stars or any of that stuff. We didn't flirt. We don't have that kind of attraction.'

Jillian piped up. 'So yours is more like an animal attraction?'

Marion shrugged. 'We liked to fuck. Luke met you, Emily. He stopped fucking me.'

'How much do you miss him?' asked Em. She gave Marion a challenging look.

'I don't. We're still pals. We live in the same house. We work together. I don't miss him, but I am overdue for a big dick up my bum!' Marion threw back her head and laughed. 'Oh Gods of Film, send me a big dick to fuck my blooming arse.'

'Something tells me you're a long way from becoming a "fair lady", Marion,' said Emily. She groaned as Jillian dug her thumbs up into her shoulders. 'What happens if I don't do it? If I just can't?'

Jillian was the first to reply. 'I'm going to make sure

my next boyfriend isn't a freak for it. He can stick a finger up there if he really wants to and I'll do the same for him. But I'm not interested in anal sex and I'm going to make that clear from the start.'

'You mean like, "Hi, my name is Jillian and I hate anal sex"?' Kara asked.

'Pretty much,' said Jillian. 'I might as well. If a couple doesn't have complementary sexual desires it's pretty much doomed, don't you think?' One hand flew from Emily's shoulder to her own mouth as she realised what she'd said.

Em's eyes filled with tears. 'Luke's not coming back here tonight,' she said. 'I think I … I think maybe Executive Producer Emily doesn't attract him the way plain old Emily did.'

'Don't be crazy. He's mad about you,' scoffed Marion. 'And you've never been plain.'

'I think you're very beautiful, Emily,' said Jillian. 'You and Marion, too,' she said to Kara. 'I mean it. I'm so happy we're friends.'

'I'd like to propose a toast to friendship but we need more wine,' said Emily. 'Jillian?'

Jillian was on her way to the basement door when it opened and the boys came trooping up.

Gary leered at Kara. 'C'mere, me saucy wench. I've sailed the seven seas and yours is the finest treasure chest I've ever laid me deadlights on.'

Kara rolled her eyes. 'Playing pirate pool?'

'Avast,' proclaimed Tony. ''Tis th' best game in th' whole world.'

Marion rose. 'There's a demonstration against the fee hikes tomorrow in the quad. We should all go. All the students on campus, not just the film students, have promised a show of solidarity. You know, today the Film Department, tomorrow – who knows? Medicine? Arts? Business?'

Emily motioned Jillian back from the door. The fun was over. She stood up, weaving a little, as much from weariness as from the wine. She felt heavy, as if there'd been a shift in the gravity of her personal space.

'We don't have any cameras any more. Luke says he's turning them in tomorrow.'

'Shit! What happened?' asked Paul.

'Ol' whatserface, Patricia, who by the way will not be returning this fall, dumped Professor Whatsisface as soon as she got her marks.'

'Simmons,' said Jillian. 'But don't worry about that, Em. I'll go visit Simmons tomorrow. When I'm done with him, he'll let us keep the cameras until school starts.'

'You'd do that? For the Movie Mob?' Marion looked shocked.

'Yeah, plus I think he's cute,' said Jillian. She giggled. 'And bad. It's not that easy to find a professor who'll exchange hand jobs for favours these days.' She wiggled her eyebrows. 'I think it's sexy.'

Tony looked at Jillian like he'd never seen her before. 'I reckon that ye thinkin' that be sort o' sexy,' he said. 'Avast.'

With that he headed for the stairs.

Paul followed.

Gary tried and failed to pick his girlfriend up in his arms.

'I need a moment, please,' Emily said to him.

'I'll wait for ye in the cabin,' he growled at his girl.

When the four girls were alone again, Emily asked the question she'd been hoping to ask all day. 'I have one script finished. Vito wants girl on girl on girl. How do the three of you feel about that?'

'I'll do it,' said Marion.

'Me too!' Jillian's eyes shone. Obviously, the attraction Emily had fancied Jillian felt for Marion was real.

'Absolutely not.'

Three pairs of astonished eyes focused on Kara.

'I don't do chicks. God, Emily. No fucking way.' Kara turned on her heel and marched to the stairs.

Once she was out of sight Marion, Jillian and Emily risked exchanging glances. As one, they clapped their hands over their mouths to stifle their giggles.

'Well,' said Emily, when she could trust herself to speak, 'I guess now we know what Kara means when she says she doesn't do kink.'

Chapter Seventeen

Luke and Richard sat at the kitchen table in their house. With the window open, they could hear the noise of the crowd protesting the Film Department's fee hike.

'Think it'll do any good?' Richard asked.

'Too little, way too late,' replied Luke. He took a swig from his coffee cup and, finding it empty, rose to fill it again. He wasn't hungover or even especially tired. He just felt a little ... old.

'We should probably go,' said Richard.

Luke sighed. He sat down at the table once more. 'Maybe. Not much point in trying to turn in the cameras today, even if we wanted to.'

'Which we don't.'

'Dunno. Em wants me to hang on to them for a while longer but I'm getting major heat from the Department.'

As if the mention of her name had summoned her, Emily's face appeared at the window. At the sight of her, Luke's heartbeat accelerated until it was pounding a tattoo in his head.

Paul and Emily came in through the kitchen door.

While Paul fetched himself a cup of coffee, Emily made a beeline for her boyfriend. 'I missed you last night,' she said.

'C'mere.' Luke patted his lap. She obliged. Luke cuddled her close, inhaling her fresh scent as if he were asthmatic and Emily the antidote. His heart stopped racing. Everything was going to be fine.

'So, did you get us a cougar?'

'Sure did,' said Richard. He leered at Emily.

Asshole. Luke gave his companion from the night before an evil look.

Richard said, 'I'm out of here,' and left by the back door.

'What's with him?' Emily wriggled in Luke's lap.

'He's going to the demonstration. I guess we should go, too.'

'Marion's there,' said Paul. He stood at the kitchen counter, sipping his coffee. He laughed. 'I asked if she'd be turning in the portable Olympus LS-100 she's always carrying and she practically tore me a new one.'

Luke smiled. 'Yeah, it's hers. She bought it as soon as it came out.'

'Nice,' said Paul. 'I dropped Jillian at the campus as well. She's gone to give the Department Head some

157

head. Or something. So we can keep the cameras until the semester starts.'

'Jesus. She hasn't even been in a porn flick and she's already whoring herself.' Luke frowned. 'Whose idea was that?' He gave Emily a piercing look.

'Hers.' Em helped herself to a sip of his coffee.

For some reason, it annoyed him. He took the mug from her hand.

'Everybody's a whore for something, sometime in their lives. Don't you think?' asked Paul. When he received no answer he picked up his cup and started to leave the kitchen. 'OK, lovebirds, if you need me I'll be –'

He was interrupted by the ring tone of Emily's cell phone. She answered. 'Hi, Marion. What? Speak up! Really? You think? OK! Yeah, I got it covered. Good idea, girlfriend.' She hung up. 'Marion says it's fantastic. She's right at the front, at the barricade set up between the protesters and the administration. It's pandemonium and she's catching it all on sound.'

'Cool,' said Paul.

'Yeah, so she wants someone to make his way through the crowd and fuck her against the barricade.'

'What? She's out of her fucking mind!' Luke stared at Emily. 'Are there cops?'

'Yeah. So? You guys go. Luke, take a hand-held camera. Paul, it's time for your close-up.'

'Wait a minute –' Paul began.

'We don't have time to argue. Just do it, OK? Go. Go!' Emily leaped from Luke's lap. She grabbed his coffee cup from his hand. 'Go!'

'What the lady wants, the lady gets,' said Luke. 'What do you think, Paul? The Samsung?'

'The Canon's smaller but for a crowd shoot you're probably –'

'Just go!' Emily was practically jumping up and down. 'This is going to be fucking fabulous!'

'Right.' Luke grabbed the Samsung. 'Bye.'

He walked out the door with Paul right behind him.

'Man, that's some bossy babe you've got, bro,' said Paul.

'Word.'

The men walked quickly towards the edge of the crowd.

'You know what Gary was sayin' last night?'

'No idea,' replied Luke.

'He says when Kara gets her panties twisted in a knot he gives her a good hard spanking.'

'No shit.'

'No shit.'

They stopped at the edge of the crowd. The cacophony of voices, some amplified by megaphones in the classic call-and-response that invited the agitated students to chant in unison, was almost overwhelming.

'One, two, three, four. We can't afford to pay no more!'

A police whistle blew and a rowdy protester was captured by cops. The crowd roared its disapproval.

Luke raised the camera. 'Marion was right about this. It's wild.' He shot the protester, who had gone limp, being dragged off to a police van. 'Don't get caught, man. I think fucking in a public place might be against the law.'

'I'm not going be doing any Marion-fucking, my friend.'

'Huh?'

Paul shook his head. 'I'm on her no-fly zone. It's in our files.'

'Fuck. Emily doesn't even look at the files any more. She just tells everyone what she wants and expects them to hop to it. Goddam it!'

'Sorry, man.'

'Please don't tell me my friend Marion is racist.'

'Nothin' like that. Depending on who you talk to, she propositioned me one night and I turned her down, which pissed her off, or I propositioned her one night and she turned me down, which pissed me off.' He grinned at Luke. 'Now you tell me, which scenario is more likely to make a little red-headed size queen permanently pissed at a poor long dong named Paul?'

'Marion does not like rejection.'

'True dat. So, I shoot, you fuck.'

Luke made a split-second decision. 'OK. Here.' He handed Paul the camera. 'It'll be fast and dirty. I'm gonna make a beeline for that sexy bitch and she sure as hell better have her panties off when I get there.'

Paul steadied the camera on his shoulder. 'At least there's a lot of press here.'

'Yeah, maybe if we're real lucky we'll make the six o'clock news.' Luke glowered.

'I mean I'll blend right in. I hope.' Paul flashed Luke another grin. 'Ready?'

'I'm more than ready. Stay close, dude. I'm gonna fuck her up the ass until she passes out from pleasure.'

'Whoa! I'm right behind you! Rolling!'

Luke started through the crowd. His blood was boiling. Little Emily who couldn't take more than a pinkie up her bum without crying like a vestal fucking virgin had whored him out *again*. Without so much as a 'would you mind, Luke?'

'Sorry,' he muttered as he trod on someone's foot. 'Man on a mission.'

As a matter of fact, Luke didn't mind at all. He hadn't had anal sex since he'd given up fucking for making love with someone so sweet he'd thought he could live without a butt fuck for the rest of his life if he had to. But 'sweet' no longer described Emily. So, if she wasn't willing to give a man what a man wanted, a man, a *real* man, would get it somewhere else.

He'd turned down a gorgeous piece of ass the night before but it hadn't been easy. He wasn't about to do it again.

The thought of sinking his dick into Marion's eager asshole was so enticing he was practically running. Paul had better keep up because he sure as hell wasn't slowing down.

She was easy to spot. Her hennaed head of riotous curls stood out even in a crowd as large and rowdy as this one. Just as she'd said, she was pressed up against the barricade, chanting along with the rest of the crowd. She'd be singing a different tune in a couple of minutes.

Marion didn't so much as look to see who it was that suddenly grabbed her from behind. She just tilted her ass back, inviting a 'stranger' to do whatever he wanted.

He unzipped his pants and flipped up her full, short skirt, exposing her bare ass for a flash. Luke gripped his dick, dipped his knees and jammed his raging hard-on up her ass. *No fuss, no muss.*

Marion gasped. She froze, both hands gripping the barricade to keep her balance as her assailant rammed the full length of his rod inside her.

'Atta girl,' he whispered. 'Take my great big dick up your ass like the anal slut you are.'

'What the hell!' Marion enunciated as best she could, given the circumstances. Obviously, she was doing her part to make sure their dialogue didn't get lost in the roar of the crowd. 'Who the fuck are you?'

'None of your business.' Luke, taking his cue from Marion, spoke as clearly as he could and as loudly as he dared. 'What the fuck difference does it make, bitch? I've got what you want. Admit it.'

He pushed harder, jamming her up against the barricade and burying his dick another quarter-inch inside her.

'I want it!'

She knew who it was. He was sure of it. Luke's memory was flooded with images of Marion and him fucking each other's brains out. It'd been so easy. So goddam fucking easy. And so much fucking fun.

'Diddle your clit if you want to come because I don't give a fuck if you do or not.'

One of Marion's hands dropped from the barricade. She wriggled it down between the barricade and her body and slid it under the hem of her skirt. She swayed a little.

Now that Luke was inside her both his hands were free. He kept one on her shoulder and grabbed the railing of the barricade with the other.

'Christ,' he hissed.

'What the hell?' A shocked voice let him know they'd been spotted. *No time to waste.*

'Hey!' This voice came from the other side of the barricade. The cops would be on him in a moment. He didn't care. If they tried to drag him off he'd drag her with him. They'd have to hose the two of them down to separate them now.

Marion moaned, 'Oh my God.'

163

Luke fucked her hard and fast. It was heaven to be inside her tight, hot little asshole. It was … it was … almost too much …

'Fuck!' The first spurt of come seemed to be sucked from his whole body, from his firmly planted feet to the top of his head.

She whimpered. 'I'm gonna come. Don't stop. Please … I'm coming right fucking now!'

Her cunt contracted so violently her tunnel squeezed the length of his prick and he spurted again and again and again and again …

Luke sunk his teeth into the back of her neck, like a mutt claiming its bitch. It was the only way he could keep from howling.

'Po-po,' muttered a voice behind him. Right. Paul.

Here came the long arm of the law.

But it didn't matter. Luke was done. He pulled out, zipped up and took off. He didn't know if Paul was behind him or had kept his camera on Marion. He didn't know and he didn't care. At the moment, he didn't even care if Marion was getting lost in the crowd or dragged off to the cop van. He was free and that's all that really mattered.

Free.

Luke didn't stop running until he was in his own back yard. He threw open the back door and practically fell into the kitchen.

Emily was exactly where he'd left her, no more than half an hour earlier. She jumped up as he burst through the door. 'What?'

'Quiet.' He glanced out the kitchen window. Nobody there. 'Ha!' Luke collapsed into a kitchen chair. He was panting like the dog he was. 'Ha!'

'Luke?'

He focused on Emily. As usual, her beauty disarmed him. He tilted his head back and closed his eyes. It would be easier if he wasn't looking at her when he spoke.

'Did you … did you guys find Marion?'

'Uh-huh.'

'Did you get the shoot?'

'Yep.'

'Great. That's terrific, Lukey.'

'You got that right.'

'What's the matter? Luke, look at me. What's going on?'

He took a deep breath and opened his eyes.

Her soft grey eyes were filled with concern. She looked innocent, as always. She smelled clean.

Innocent and clean, while he was sordid and dirty. Last night he'd eaten out an older woman and shoved a vibrator up her butt while she rode his buddy's dick. His first threesome had been forced on him by his own girlfriend. Fifteen minutes ago, he'd fucked his roommate up the ass in full view of his peers and professors, again at Emily's orders. And there she sat, fresh as a fucking daisy. It made him mad.

She leaned forwards to touch his knee. 'Talk to me.'

'Don't touch me, please,' he said in an even tone.

Emily's hand jerked back as if he'd smacked it. 'Oh God, what is it? Did someone get arrested? What happened, Luke? Talk to me!'

'Talk to you? OK, Emily, since you asked so nice. I'll talk to you. Let's see – I'm very tired. I'd like some alone time now.'

'We are alone, Lukey. Let's go upstairs.' Emily stood.

'I mean all alone. I want you to go back to your house and leave me be for a bit.'

'No. Not until I get some answers.' Emily folded her arms.

The little bitch.

'I'm the one looking for answers, Emily, and you better have them ready for me when I see you again.'

'What's that supposed to mean?' She planted her feet. Her face began to turn red.

'Hey!' His voice was sharp. 'Don't even think of pulling one of your tantrums on me, little girl.'

Emily recoiled instantly. She whispered, 'What's happening?'

'Dunno.' Luke stood. He folded his arms, imitating her. 'But here's what's going to happen. Listen up because I'm only saying it once. I'm going up to my room. I'm going to get my black belt. The thick one. You know the one I mean?'

'Uh-huh.'

'I'm going to bring that belt right here, to the kitchen. And if you're still here, Emily, I'm going to put you over my knee and spank your ass until it's covered in welts. Until you beg me to stop. I don't care how much noise you make, or who sees us, or how hard you struggle. I'm going to take my belt to your ass and teach you a lesson you won't forget.'

Her mouth fell open. She stared at him as if he were a stranger. 'B-b-b-but –'

'I'm leaving the kitchen now, Em. Going to get my thick black belt. If you think you'd like to sit down sometime this week, you'd better get moving. Otherwise I swear to … to the Gods of Film, I am going to beat your ass black and blue.'

Luke sauntered out of the kitchen. He climbed the stairs at a leisurely pace. In his room, he opened his closet door and selected the black leather belt from among a few others hanging on hooks on the inside of the door. He doubled it and smacked it hard against his palm. The sound was satisfying. His palm stung. This would do nicely.

He descended the stairs, again taking his time. He didn't know if he hoped she'd be there or not. On the one hand, it would be immensely satisfying to punish her for the thoughtless way she'd cheapened their relationship. The way she'd cheapened *him*. On the other hand, if he beat her the way he'd said he would, the way he fully intended to if she was still in the kitchen, then she'd be cheapened, too. She'd never seem clean to him again and that would be a terrible pity.

The kitchen was empty.

Luke shoved the belt through the loops of his jeans and buckled it. From now on, he'd make sure he was wearing it whenever he saw Emily.

If, that is, he ever saw her again.

Chapter Eighteen

Three days had passed. Emily sat at the desk in her father's study. It was a place she'd rarely visited since his death, four years ago. When she'd returned from Luke's house she'd gathered up all her executive producer materials, come in here and started sorting them out. Hopefully, it would help her find the answers Luke was looking for.

He'd been so angry. And that belt – the one he'd so calmly announced he'd beat her with if she was still in his kitchen when he returned – it was thick black leather. Smooth on the outside but rough, unfinished leather on the inside. Emily shuddered.

Daddy had never spanked her. Tears filmed her eyes. Here she was, an orphan, practically, just trying to do her best by everyone and she'd fucked up royally. *Mama!* Was it her birth mother she yearned for, the one she couldn't remember? Or Bobby, who'd only been trying to do what Daddy had told her to do in his will?

The first night after 'the incident' she'd searched in

vain for information about Bobby's relatives in Brazil. Emily had never shown any interest in who they were or where they lived. Brazil was a place she'd visit with Bobby, maybe, someday, after she finished school ... damn! Maybe that was the answer Luke was looking for? Emily was self-centred? She'd made a note.

The next day she'd gone through the fact sheets on the Movie Mob. Sure enough, Kara's stated clearly that she didn't do girls. Worse, though, were Marion's preferences. She wanted to work in sound: recording it and marrying it to the finished movie. She wanted to write. She wanted to act and was willing to play with anyone, male or female, *except Paul*. How long had Emily been operating on 'instinct', deciding who should do what, regardless of what they'd stated they wanted to do? Add to that the fact that she'd been shooting and releasing movies all summer without issuing a single contract to her 'people'. The only contract that mattered, she'd decided early on, was the one she'd signed with Vito. So she'd provided shelter and food for them and ignored their increasingly frequent requests for more than the allowance she'd doled out each week. She'd treated them like children, all the while denouncing Bobby for treating her the same way. But –

Emily glanced around the room, taking in the Geological diplomas and maps and photos she'd admired all her life. Her vision blurred. Lung cancer had killed her dad and while Bobby blamed 'those damned devil sticks', the cigarettes he'd smoked, Emily had always clung to the belief that he'd died of black lung, the miner's disease, because he was always down in the mines, making sure the mines were safe and the miners were treated well. He'd prided himself on that.

Pride. Emily had made another note. She'd planned to throw a big party, once she had the money to pay everyone's tuition increase. She'd imagined doling out cheques to the grateful employees of NAIL when in fact they didn't work for NAIL, they *were* NAIL.

She'd paid the graphic artist his asking price, after haggling with him all summer, for the gorgeous NAIL Productions Limited logo he'd created. She'd paid the bands Marion had chosen from the demo discs Eric had provided. She'd paid the huge amount NAIL owed the clinic where cast and crew received their monthly PCR/ DNA tests.

Next, Emily had fished Vito's sample contract from the pile of paperwork she'd ignored all summer. It had been easy enough to draw up contracts and issue cheques to the people living in her house, but she hadn't seen anyone who lived in the house on campus except Richard. He'd tried to sneak in and drop off the first short of the 'Strangers' series – Marion at the student demonstration – without being caught. But Emily had cornered him.

Now, she almost laughed at the way he'd stuttered

and stumbled his way through his explanation of exactly how he and Luke had found their cougar. *Fuck*. He kept reminding her that she'd told Luke to do whatever he had to do to get an older woman for their shoot. She'd squeezed the truth out of him, trapping him with questions that expressed concern for everyone's wellbeing. Did this … this Gloria woman have papers that proved she was free of STIs? 'Oh yeah, we made sure of it. She takes the same test we do, every month. I felt perfectly safe.' And Luke? Had he felt safe, too? Richard had rushed to reassure her. 'Absolutely. Luke was just as comfortable as me.' Only then had Richard realised what he'd done.

Emily's hands balled into fists. Gloria was supposed to arrive this afternoon for the cougar shoot and when she walked through the door Emily would pound her to – Her own words came back to haunt her: 'Go get a cougar … I don't care what it takes.'

She made a series of notes in increasingly large, illegible print. *Idiot. Power hungry. Fucking rude. Thoughtless. Careless. Bad.*

After Richard had left she'd watched the short. Luke, her Luke, shoving his way through the crowd to the barrier at the front. Barking his 'lines' at Marion while he unzipped his pants and stuck his raging hard-on up that red-headed slut's ass. On the one hand, it was porno gold. On the other hand, it was heartbreaking. 'Go. Just go!' she'd ordered Luke and Paul. But Marion didn't do

Paul. Luke … well, obviously the size queen anal whore had no qualms about doing him.

It was a good thing she'd finished the contracts by then because she'd run straight up the stairs to her room, getting there just in time to puke her guts out in her bathroom. She'd thrown herself on her bed and covered her head with a pillow to muffle her screams.

Kara and Jillian let themselves in, though she'd yelled at them to stay away. She'd confessed all. She'd begged Kara to send Gary to get Luke and Kara had done so, while Jillian stroked her hair and rubbed her shoulders and gently washed her face.

Finally, she'd sobbed herself to sleep, sure that when she awoke Luke would be there to hold her. To forgive her. Fuck, to beat her with his belt if that's what it would take to get him back.

But it hadn't turned out that way at all.

Now, she heard the unmistakable sound of Paul's old car pulling up to the house. Thank God! They were shooting that fucking cougar this afternoon and she'd held on to the hope that professionalism would force them to show up. Richard and Paul got out of the car, each loaded with equipment. She waited, though it was obvious the car was now empty. No Luke. No Marion, either.

Jillian knocked at the door of the study and opened it. 'Honey, I've got to dress the set.'

Emily nodded. She gathered her papers together

carefully, but before she tucked them into her soft-sided briefcase she added one more word to her list: *Hopeless*.

Chapter Nineteen

A dozen cables snaked up the staircase and into Emily's bedroom. Emily crept up, planting her feet carefully. They were supposed to be shooting the *Sleepover* sequence in her bedroom but it didn't sound like it.

Half the room was still pink and white and frilly, kept by Bobby like a shrine ever since Emily had left. The other half was cluttered with lights and filters and reflectors; sound equipment, apple boxes, gels and their two cameras, one static, on a tripod, the other mounted on a rubber-wheeled dolly. The crew, Richard, Tony and Gary, was standing around, idle. Luke was sitting in his director's chair, shuffling papers on a bar stool he was using as an improvised desk. He did not look happy. He *was* wearing his heavy leather belt.

The sight of it made Emily tremble.

She'd texted her list of personal failings to him and asked him to come to direct the *Sleepover* piece. His reply, also by text, had been a simple 'OK'. She hadn't been quite sure if that meant she was forgiven but the mere knowledge that she'd see him the next day had been enough to raise her spirits.

She'd slept in Bobby's room last night so her room could be dressed for the shoot. To her chagrin, she'd been so relieved she'd slept like the dead, missing Luke's arrival and the prep for the shoot by several hours. A call to her cell from Vito had finally roused her. People were clamouring for more NAIL movies. He wondered when she'd be delivering new product.

Emily wondered the same thing.

There'd been no time to waste primping for what she hoped would be her reunion with Luke. Instead, she'd simply set the rest of the Movie Mob to work, preparing the main floor for the first scene of the long awaited *Pool Party* shoot and then headed up the stairs to check on the progress of *Sleepover*.

Emily didn't want to greet Luke like the wacky E.P. of NAIL; she wanted to greet him like a contrite girlfriend. So she waited patiently until he finally decided to acknowledge her arrival by glancing in her direction.

'Hi,' she said.

'Hello, Emily,' he replied.

'Problem?'

'You don't know?'

'No. What?'

'Aileen phoned from Vancouver. She has the flu. Can't make it. That leaves us with two girls for our threesome. We're ready. Everything is set up. All we're missing is one more female body.'

'Fu– for crying out loud. We don't have another girl!'

'Nope.' He threw a fistful of papers down. 'Our two girls, Marion and Jillian, are pretty flexible about who they'd do but that doesn't help now, does it! Jillian's first choice was Marion.'

'How about Marion's first choice? I don't remember ...'

'Why does that not surprise me?'

Em shrugged. She'd worked hard over the last few days. In fact she had a contract and cheque for Luke in her briefcase and the same for Marion and Jillian. They were the last members of NAIL left to be paid, except for herself. Unfortunately, Em wouldn't be paid a penny because NAIL had no more money.

If Luke wanted to keep punishing her for not paying attention to the details of cast and crew there was nothing more she could do about it. She started to toss her head but stopped herself in time. *No pride, Emily. Not now.* It was fucking impossible to be a contrite girlfriend and a professional E.P. at the same time. But she was damn well gonna keep trying!

'Marion wrote a name in, but not that of one of the talent,' he said.

'Who then?'

'You.'

'Me?' That was a stunner.

'Remember now? Or are you still in denial about your deep dark desire to make out with chicks?'

'Oh, Luke! Stop it.' Emily fished his contract and cheque out of her briefcase. That'd give him something to do while she figured out what *she* should do next.

He barely looked at the paperwork. 'Thanks.'

'Everyone's being paid today,' she said.

'Great. So? Time's a-wasting.'

'Just give me a moment to think,' she muttered.

'Whatever it takes,' Luke reminded her.

'I know, Luke.'

'By the way, I'm sorry about Gloria. She didn't seem like a drunk the night she and Richard and I ... met.'

'She showed up hammered at two in the afternoon. We had to send her away in a cab.'

'What did she have to say about that?'

'She said, quite distinctly for someone so smashed, "We are not amused."'

Luke laughed. 'Crazy English bitch. Anyway, I imagine NAIL needs this girlie shoot?'

'Desperately.'

'Emily, it's simple. Is it or is it not time for your close-up?'

'I need a minute.'

Luke shrugged. He stood, hooked his thumbs into his belt loops and ambled off to confer with his crew.

Emily sank into his director's chair, then quickly jumped up. Nobody sits in the director's chair but the director. So. Pros and cons. That's the way to make important decisions. On the pro side, the show had to go on. On the same side, she'd been wondering about her own sexuality ever since NAIL had started. If she *was* bi, this would be one way to find out – in a movie, though, which was definitely a con.

That goddam mind-blowing ass-fuck between Marion and Luke had practically driven Emily insane. How did she feel about making love to a girl who'd fucked her man, on camera no less? Was that a downer, or did it add spice? The only way to find out would be to try it.

And then there was Luke. She'd kinda, accidentally, not meaning to, encouraged him to screw that useless cougar Gloria, and then she'd done it again, pushing him into screwing Marion, in public no less! That just wasn't reasonable. Now, Luke was challenging her to appear on camera, in an all-girl scene that featured Marion as one of the players. Was he just trying to punish her? Or would that make it even-steven? One thing was for sure, if Luke got to watch her make out with another girl – two other girls, actually – it'd drive him crazy, in a good way. Would his lust heal their relationship? If he wanted her badly enough, would that make him forgive her?

Goddam right it would!

Emily called, 'OK,' quickly, before she could change her mind.

Luke returned, thumbs still hooked in the loops of his jeans.

Emily almost laughed. *Yes, dear, I see your scary black belt.*

'You'll take direction from me?' he asked.

'Of course.'

Luke grinned.

It melted her heart. Her eyes filled with tears, but he wasn't looking at her, he was looking at the script. She blinked hard. Time to put on a new hat – that of the actress.

Luke explained the scene to her in detail, even though she'd written it. She nodded and asked questions as if every word he said was liquid gold.

'So I'm playing Abby?'

'Yes. Marion is Connie. Jillian will be Babs. How come their names start with A and B and C?'

'Writers' reasons. Movie Magic Screenwriter remembers names for you. If they all have different initials, a name becomes a single keystroke.'

'Huh. Saves time.'

She willed him to look at her but he kept his eyes on the script.

'Abby gets the shirt, right?' Emily asked.

'It's waiting for you in the make-up–wardrobe room, not that you need make-up.'

'On screen, we all need make-up.' That was nice, what

he'd said, especially since he knew better. He had to be warming to her already.

Marion and Jillian were doing each other's make-up when Emily walked in. Jillian took off, powder puff in hand. Marion's face blushed neon pink.

'I'm sorry,' she said. 'You can hit me if you want but I'm supposed to be on camera any minute. Unless I'm fired.'

'You don't have anything to apologise for,' said Emily. 'Everything that's gone wrong is my fault.' She handed Marion a contract with a cheque clipped to it. 'This is long overdue.'

'Thanks, Em.' Marion glanced at the cheque. 'Wow. Thanks again!'

Emily shrugged. 'You earned every penny.'

Jillian peeked around the door. 'Is it safe?'

'Silly,' said Emily. 'Get in here.'

She handed Jillian her paperwork. Now everyone's fee hike had been covered, except her own. But they didn't need to know that.

Twenty minutes later, Luke called, 'Action!'

The three girls giggled off camera for a count of three and then ran onto the set to throw themselves on to the double bed. Emily, playing Abby, wore a man's crisp blue shirt, buttoned most of the way up. Marion, as Connie, sprawled in a pair of pink satin pyjamas. Jillian, as Babs, was a throwback to the 50s in a peek-a-boo babydoll made of chiffon and lace. She was the only one who was showing much skin, apart from Abby's long slender legs. The top was transparent and cropped, so her nipples were almost visible and there was plenty of midriff on display above her frilly panties.

Babs said, 'Abby, it's so good of your folks to let us a have a sleepover while they're gone. When will they be back, anyway?'

'Not till morning, earliest. They've gone to see *Turandot.*'

'An opera,' Connie explained when Babs drew a blank.

Abby continued, 'They've gone with another couple and are going back to their place for "drinkies" after. They'll sleep over and come home tomorrow.'

Babs gave her a knowing look. 'Two couples, sleeping over? I wonder who will be sleeping with who?'

Abby slapped her friend's thigh. 'Don't be ridiculous. They're way past that sort of thing.'

Connie raised an eyebrow. 'Past it, in their forties? Don't you believe it, Abby.'

'Change the subject,' Abby snapped.

'OK.' Babs giggled. 'How about Truth, Dare and Consequences?'

'That's a kids' game,' Abby complained.

'It doesn't have to be. You play ping-pong, don't you, Abby?'

'Ping-pong? What's that got to do ...?'

'Get me a paddle and I'll explain.'

Abby leaped up and out of shot, deliberately flashing her legs at the static camera. She returned with a paddle in her hand. 'So? Now what?'

Connie gave the paddle a knowing look. 'I think I can guess.'

'Chicken?' Babs asked.

'Not so far.'

'Explain, one of you,' Abby demanded.

Babs took the paddle from Abby. 'This makes me Queen. I pick one of you and ask her "Truth, or dare?" She takes the paddle and asks a question of the last of us, or makes a dare. For example,' she told Abby, 'truth. Now you ask Connie a question, a good one.'

'I get it. Connie, did you ever kiss a boy?'

The other two laughed. Connie said, 'Me? Never!'

'I don't believe you.'

'Me neither,' Babs added, 'so you have to take the consequences, Connie. On your tummy.'

Connie rolled over.

'Bare your tush!'

Giggling, Connie hooked her thumbs into the waist of her pj pants and eased them down.

Babs took the paddle and gave her friend a whack on the left cheek of her bottom before passing it to Abby, who followed suit on Connie's right cheek.

'Now Connie is Queen,' Babs explained.

Connie took the paddle and said, 'Babs. Truth.'

Babs asked Abby, 'How many girls have you kissed, real kisses, not pecks? French kisses, with tongues?'

'Two. I was a bit tipsy both times. It was quick, both times. Hardly counts. My turn as Queen?'

Over the next few turns it was established that all three of them had kissed other girls at least twice, had enjoyed it and would do it again, with the right girl. Connie was accused of blatant, deliberate lies, twice, and got paddled each time. The second time she didn't pull her pants up, after, though she stayed on her tummy.

Dimly, past the glare of the lights, Emily saw Luke signal for them to move it along. She also got the impression that he had an enormous erection trapped in his jeans.

Connie dared Abby to take her panties off.

'Gotcha! I'm not wearing any.'

'Then you won't?'

'Can't.'

'That's no excuse. On your tummy.'

Emily, in her role as Abby, obeyed, both acting and feeling reluctant. She'd written this scene so she could hardly chicken out but ...

Someone lifted her shirt at the back. She closed her eyes. 'Ouch! That hurt.' It did, too. The second smack came down even harder. Fuck! It burned, but it wasn't unbearable. In fact ...

As she'd written it, when she got the chance, she, as Abby, dared Babs to unbutton Connie's pj top. Connie sat up with her top loose and open. She had really cute tits. With them bare and her pj pants pushed halfway down her thighs, she had a sexy dishevelled look that Emily had hoped would turn the viewers on. It certainly seemed to have that effect on her, that is, Abby, her character ... *Focus!*

Next round, Connie dared Babs to take Abby's shirt off. That left Abby naked, Connie half-bare and Babs still covered by her see-through babydoll. The dolly camera tracked and dipped, coming in for close-ups that would be intercut with the relatively static shoot from the tripod camera.

In the script, Emily had written: 'BY NOW, THE GIRLS ARE REALLY TURNED ON. THE GAME IS BEING USED AS A FLIMSY EXCUSE FOR GETTING IT ON IN EARNEST.'

That was true, not only of the characters but of the actresses playing them. Emily's question about her own sexuality – was she bi or not? – had been pretty much answered. Was that going to complicate things with Luke? Or was watching her make out with two other girls turning Luke on so much that he'd forget their quarrel?

Damn fucking right it was!

Babs had barely got her dare to Abby to kiss Connie out before the two girls had their tongues in each other's mouths. The paddle was tossed from hand to hand. Everyone got to kiss everyone and admit the truth, that they loved it. Breasts were caressed; nipples were tweaked and sucked.

Emily became lost in her character; she was Abby, a little scared and very intrigued. She enunciated her scripted lines for the benefit of the sound man and posed for the cameras but the emotions she expressed, with those words and her body, were real.

She was dared, by Connie, to kiss Connie's navel. If she had any doubts left about making it with girls, this was approaching the ultimate test. Abby had barely twirled the tip of her tongue into Connie's intimate dimple when Babs pulled Connie's pj pants the rest of the way off and pushed down on the top of Abby's head.

Here goes!

Connie fell back and spread her thighs. Abby's head nestled between them. Mm. Pussy didn't taste at all bad.

Abby was distracted by Connie toppling sideways and raising her thigh so as not to trap Abby's head. From the corner of her eye, Abby could make out why. Babs had sprawled out the same way, offering the inside of her thigh to Connie as a pillow. All that left was …

Abby's own thigh was urged up so that Babs' warm wet tongue could squirm into the folds of her pussy.

In that erotic triangle, the three girls followed the

script, sighing, moaning and softly squealing. They flexed and twitched as if electrified with lust.

Luke signalled.

Their reactions grew wilder. Emily discovered that faking being turned on uncontrollably actually turned her on.

Luke signalled, emphatically.

Damn! Another few minutes and she'd have got there, but the shoot comes first. She screamed into Connie's cunt. All three shook convulsively before falling apart, onto their backs, looks of utter bliss on their juice-drenched faces.

Luke said, 'Cut. Well done, people. That's a wrap. Emily, we need to … um … talk. Come with me.'

He took her hand and pulled her up. His erection brushed her hip. *Talk? Yeah, right!*

As he tugged her down the stairs, presumably to Bobby's bedroom, he used his free hand to begin undoing the buckle of his thick leather belt.

No! Despite herself, Emily broke free and leaped downstairs two at a time, with Luke close behind. 'I'm not ready!' she shrieked. She hit the landing and ran through the living room, dancing nimbly over the cables that led to the back yard. 'Lukey, wait,' she cried, laughing so hard her words were barely words at all.

'I know what I'm doing!' Luke was in hot pursuit. He tugged the belt free of his pants. 'Gary gave me lessons!'

'Help!' was Emily's response.

The tip of the belt connected with the bottom swell of her ass. It stung like a bitch.

'Help!' Emily shrieked at the top of her lungs as she fled to the back yard.

She flew into the arms of the first person she saw, hitting the woman so hard both she and Bobby tumbled into the pool.

Bobby?

Chapter Twenty

'Fuck me!'

Luke barely had time to put his belt back on before Bobby, drenched and furious, ascended the ladder from the pool and came at him, her long nails curled into claws.

'Bastard! I will kill you!' Her thin shift clung to her curves.

Fuck, what a bodacious babe. 'We were just fooling around. Honest!' Luke backed away from his assailant. He covered his face with his hands, elbows out to deflect his attacker.

'My baby does not run about naked and screaming. You sadistic rapist!' Bobby raked her claws down his bare arm.

Despite himself, and the pain, Luke started to laugh. *What a fucking disaster!*

Bobby curled her hands into fists. She popped him a good one on his left temple. 'You think it is funny to try and kill my Emily? I will kill you!'

'I can explain!' Luke, dizzy from the blow to his head, tripped over a patio chair and fell. 'Emily! Help!'

Bobby, poised to leap on top of him, glanced at the pool, where Emily had yet to surface.

Luke took advantage of the diversion to leap to his feet and run. He raced around the pool as fast as he could, given that he was dizzy and the poolside area was crowded with NAIL members in various stages of déshabille.

'Emily!' Bobby screamed at the pool. 'What are you doing?'

Probably trying to grow gills. Luke laughed again. *At least he'd die a happy man.*

Emily surfaced at last. She stayed in the middle of the pool, dog paddling her heart out while coughing and sputtering. 'B-Bobby! What are you doing here?'

'What am I doing? This is my home. What are you doing? Who are these people? Get out of the pool, right this minute, or I will come back in and get you myself.'

'I'm ... I'm coming.' Emily swam as slowly as possible to the ladder. 'Don't hurt me.'

'Me?' Bobby pointed at Luke. 'He is chasing you and you are naked and screaming for help and you ask *me* not to hurt you?'

'I can explain.' Emily reluctantly climbed out of the pool.

'Everybody can explain but nobody does!' Bobby grabbed a towel and threw it at Emily. 'Cover yourself!'

Luke cowered behind Eric. 'Hurry, Em! She's trying to kill me!'

Kara, clad only in a skimpy bikini bottom, coolly observed the goings-on. She broke into a smile as some of the *Sleepover* cast and crew cautiously stepped through the open doorway. 'Gary! We've got drama. *Real* drama!'

'Cool,' said Gary. He walked around the poolside to Kara's chaise longue and slid in beside her. To make matters worse, he nonchalantly kissed each of her nipples.

Marion and Jillian, still in their costumes from the shoot, gaped at Bobby.

'Is this our new cougar?' Jillian asked.

'No! This is my mommy,' cried Emily. She threw her arms around Bobby and hugged her hard. 'I figured out why I've resisted all your hugs and kisses, Bobby.'

'Oh my God!' Bobby's eyes rolled heavenward. 'Daniel, it is my fault. I made you move her from her happy home in Philadelphia, her friends, her school, even the grave of her real mother, so I could be gawking at movie stars.' She tried to beat her breast but Emily was wrapped around her so tight it was impossible. Instead, she stroked the wet girl's blonde hair.

'I don't remember it,' said Emily. She gazed into Bobby's eyes. 'I don't remember her. *You* are my mother.'

'I try to hug and kiss you, like my mama hugs and kisses me. But I am from Brazil, where every mother and daughter behave like this. Even when I go there, this time, I put my head on my mama's big bosom and cry. It helps me. It is just our way, my darling. But it is not *your* way. Forgive me.'

'I've always loved your hugs,' said Emily. 'It's just that they made me feel … strange. But now I know why! It's not because your behaviour was inappropriate. It's because I wasn't ready to face the truth about myself.'

Fuck. Luke almost regretted the call he'd made to Aileen, telling her to put off her return to LA for a few days. He'd been trying to help Emily realise something he'd long suspected. He'd hoped it would help their future as a couple to accept that it was OK if they couldn't give each other everything, sexually, as long as they were honest and careful and open about it. Although maybe not *this* open?

'And what is this truth?'

No, Emily. Luke peered around the barrier of Eric's beefy back. He focused on Emily, trying to send her a telepathic message. *Not now.*

'I'm bisexual!' Emily announced gaily.

'Oh my God! And these are your bisexual friends?' Bobby made a sweeping gesture with one hand, still clinging to Emily with the other.

'Well, they are,' said Emily, indicating Marion and Jillian. 'But most of these people are part of my – don't freak out, now – my film company. NAIL Productions Limited.'

'Nail? Like a nail to hang a picture on. Or a fingernail?'

Like the ones that scratched my arm. 'Em? Sweetheart?' Luke risked attracting attention to himself. 'Why don't we all settle down with some drinks, maybe whip up some nachos? Have a little break before –'

Emily shook her head. 'She has to know, Luke.' She stepped back from Bobby as Jillian approached with a short pink terry cover-up. For a moment, as Emily dropped the towel and slipped into the cover-up, she was nude. 'Naked and In Love,' she said. 'I'm the executive producer of a porn company.'

Bobby swayed on the spot. She pressed the knuckles of her left hand to her forehead.

Richard stepped through the doorway. He carried a stack of plastic glasses and a pitcher of sangria on a tray, which he almost dropped when he spotted Bobby.

'Hey,' he said. He put the tray down on a patio table. 'The Rose of Brazil! We're supposed to meet tomorrow. What are you doing here?'

Bobby stared at him.

Emily stared at Bobby.

Luke stared at Emily. He loved her so much it almost hurt, especially at times like this, when she was vulnerable and confused. *Fuck it.* Luke started walking towards his girlfriend and her stepmother, the Rose of … *What the fuck?*

Chapter Twenty-one

'I think you are mistaken,' said Bobby.

Emily's eyes narrowed. Bobby looked like a trapped, drowned rat. Em almost felt sorry for her. *Almost.* Emily looked from Bobby to Richard and back again. 'What's this?'

'Remember when I asked you if I could try and track down some of the porn stars that disappeared early in their careers?'

'Yes,' replied Em.

Richard poured a glass of sangria and handed it to Bobby. 'Well, I found one – The Rose of Brazil. We're supposed to meet tomorrow, at The Muggery.'

Luke slid his arm around Emily. She leaned against him with a sigh so deep it was practically a shudder. He was her safety net. Her shelter. Her love. She saw the scratches on his other arm. Any lingering pity for Bobby vanished.

'You said you were coming home at Christmas,' she

said to Bobby. 'Yet here you are at the end of August. What's up? A job offer?'

'I don't think so,' repeated Bobby. She began to shiver. 'I think I am jet-lagging.'

'Hmm. It would explain a lot. Like why Daddy hated the film business.'

Jillian produced another terry wrap. She held it open for Bobby.

'The Rose of Brazil has a tattoo of a rose on her hip,' said Richard.

'You know I have no tattoo,' said Bobby. 'You have seen me naked many times.'

'Not completely naked,' replied Emily. 'Take your dress off, Bobby. Put on that nice terry robe. Don't be afraid.'

'Fine.' Bobby lifted her shift by the hem up and over her head. She threw the wet garment aside. As usual, she was braless, wearing only bikini panties.

'Oooh, that's a bingo,' cooed Richard.

'Thank you, Mr *Inglourious Basterd*,' Bobby said.

Richard swooned.

Bobby tugged her panties down and off. A tiny rose tattoo adorned the inside of her left hip.

'Happy?' she asked her stepdaughter.

'Yes,' Emily replied.

'We have our cougar!' crowed Richard.

'Praise be to the Gods of Film!' shouted Paul.

NAIL Productions Limited broke into wild applause. Wolf whistles pierced the air.

'Daniel,' said Bobby, rolling her eyes upward one last time. 'I. Tried.' She donned her robe, sat down at the patio table and sipped her drink. 'So, we shall be a porn star family?'

Emily sat beside her. 'For a while. We'll see what happens. As long as we're a family.'

A little smile crossed Bobby's lips. 'OK. But no funny business for you and me together. Understand?'

'Yes, Mommy,' said Emily. It made her laugh to see the pleasure Bobby took from this small triumph.

'Luke,' said Bobby. 'Sit. I think I will not kill you after all. Perhaps you will be part of my family soon?'

Luke sat beside Emily. 'Yep,' he said.

Someone slid a disc into a boombox. The Zouk-Lambada music inspired Kara and Gary to get up and dance. Jillian and Marion produced chips and dip from the kitchen. Eric fired up the grill. It looked like NAIL was having a real pool party. The *Pool Party* shoot would have to wait.

Emily saw Eric and Bobby lock eyes for a moment, which surprised her. Still, Bobby had been alone for a long time. As long as Emily had Luke, she was happy. If she and Marion had the occasional play date, well, Marion and Luke probably would, too. And then there was Jillian. She sighed with contentment.

'Lukey,' she whispered, 'were you really going to spank me with that belt?'

'Nope,' he whispered back. 'I'm not going to spank you at all. At least, not until you ask me to.'

She shivered, although she was anything but cold.

Luke cupped her cheek and pressed his lips to hers. The kiss told her everything she needed to know. At least, almost everything.

When the kiss ended, she said, 'Say those three little words, please.'

'I'll do anything for you, Emily. You know that, right?'

'Yes.'

'Lights,' he whispered in her ear.

She wriggled with delight.

'Camera,' Luke continued.

'Mm. More,' Emily pleaded.

'Action!'